Mary Elizabeth Braddon

Asphodel

Vol. 1

Mary Elizabeth Braddon

Asphodel
Vol. 1

ISBN/EAN: 9783337050078

Printed in Europe, USA, Canada, Australia, Japan

Cover: Foto ©Andreas Hilbeck / pixelio.de

More available books at **www.hansebooks.com**

ASPHODEL

A Novel

BY THE AUTHOR OF

"LADY AUDLEY'S SECRET"

ETC. ETC. ETC.

In Three Volumes

VOL. I.

LONDON

JOHN AND ROBERT MAXWELL

MILTON HOUSE, SHOE LANE, FLEET STREET

1881

CHARLES DICKENS AND EVANS,
CRYSTAL PALACE PRESS.

Dedication.

———

Dear Lady Londesborough,

I have great pleasure in taking advantage of your kind permission to inscribe this book to you, and in acknowledging the generous interest you have taken in the progress of the story, and in those pages in which I have faintly sketched that charming retreat within whose hospitable walls I have spent so many happy hours. Pray accept my grateful recollections, and allow me to remain,

Ever sincerely yours,

THE AUTHOR.

Lichfield House, Richmond, Surrey,
January, 1881.

CONTENTS TO VOL. I.

ASPHODEL.

CHAPTER I.

"AND SHE WAS FAIR AS IS THE ROSE IN MAY."

"OH, you glorious old Sol, how I love you!" cried Daphne.

It was a day on which common mortals were almost fainting with the heat, puffing and blowing and complaining—a blazing midsummer day; and even here in the forest of Fontainebleau, where the mere idea of innumerable trees was suggestive of shadow and coolness, the heat was barely supportable—a heavy slumberous heat, loud with the hum of millions of insects, perfumed with the breath of a thousand pines.

VOL. I.   B

Daphne revelled in the fierce sunshine—she threw back her crest of waving hair, bright as yellow gold, she smiled up at the cloudless blue, she looked unwinkingly even at Sol himself, the mighty unquenchable king of the sky, glorious yonder in his highest heaven.

She was lying at full length on a moss-grown block of stone at the top of a hill which was one of the highest points in the forest, a hill-top over-looking on one side a fair sweep of champagne country, fertile valleys, church steeples, village roofs, vineyards and rose gardens, and winding streams; and on the other side, woodlands stretch-ing away into infinite distance, darkly purple.

It was the choicest spot in a forest which, at its best, is a poor thing compared with the immemorial growth of an old English wood. Here there are no such oaks and beeches as our Hampshire forest can show—no such lovely mystical glades—no such richness of undergrowth. Everything seems of yesterday, save here and there a tree that looks as if he had seen something of bygone generations, and here and there a wreck of an ancient oak, proudly labelled The Great Pharamond, or *Le Chêne de Henri IV.*, with a placard hung round his poor old neck to say that he is not to be damaged "on pain of amend." Such Pharamonds and Henris abound in the forest where Rufus was killed, and nobody heeds them. The owls build in them, the field-mice find shelter in them, the woodpecker taps at them, unscared by placards or the threat of an amend.

But in the Fontainebleau woods there are rocky glades which English forests cannot boast—wild walks between walls of gigantic granite boulders—queer shapes of monsters and animals in gray stone, which seem to leap out at one from the shadows as one passes; innumerable pine-trees; hills and hollows; pathways carpeted with red fir-needles, mosses, ferns, and wild flowers; and a bluer, brighter sky than the heaven which roofs an English landscape.

"Isn't this worlds better than Asnières?" asked Daphne of her companion; "and aren't you ever so grateful to those poor girls for catching scarlet-fever?"

Asnières was school and constraint, Fontaine-bleau was liberty; so if the forest had been a poorer place, Daphne, who hated all restraints, would have loved it.

"Poor girls!" sighed Martha Dibb, a stupid, honest-minded young person, whose father kept an Italian warehouse in New Oxford Street, and whose mother had been seized with the aspiration to have her daughters finished at Continental schools; whereby one Miss Dibb was being half-starved upon sausage and cabbage at Hanover, while the other grew fat upon *croûte au pot* and *bouilli* in the neighbourhood of Paris, and was supposed to be acquiring the true Parisian accent. "Poor girls; it was very bad for them," sighed Martha.

"Yes; but it was very good for us," answered Daphne lightly; "and if it was a part of their destiny to have scarlet-fever, how very nice of them to have it in the term instead of in the holidays, when we shouldn't have profited by it."

"And how lucky that we had that good-natured Miss Toby sent with us instead of one of the French governesses."

"Lucky, indeed!" cried Daphne, with her bright laugh. "That good simple Toby, with whom we can do exactly what we like, and who is the image of quiet contentment, so long as she has even the stupidest novel to read, and some acid-drops to suck. I tremble when I think of the amount of acid-drops she must consume in the course of a year."

"Why do you give her so many?" asked the practical Martha.

"They are my peace-offerings when I have been especially troublesome," said Daphne, with the air of a sinner who gloried in her troublesome-ness. "Poor dear old Toby! if I were to give her a block of sweetstuff as tall as King Cheops's pyramid, it wouldn't atone for the life I lead her."

"I hope she won't get into trouble with Madame for letting us run wild like this," suggested Miss Dibb doubtfully.

"How should Madame know anything about it? And do you think she would care a straw if she did?" retorted Daphne. "She will get paid

exactly the same for us whether we are roaming
at large in this lovely old forest, or grinding at
grammar, and analysis, and Racine, and Lafontaine
in the stuffy schoolroom at Asnières, where the
train goes shrieking over the bridge every half-hour
carrying happy people to Paris and gaiety, and
theatres and operas, and all the good things of this
life. What does Madame Tolmache care, so long as
we are out of mischief? And I don't see how we can
get into any mischief here, unless that lovely green
lizard we saw darting up the gray rock just now
should turn into an adder and sting us to death."

"If Miss Toby hadn't a headache we couldn't
have come out without her," said Martha musingly.

"May Toby and her headache flourish! If she
had been well enough to come with us we should
have been crawling along the dusty white road at
the edge of the forest, and should never have got
here. Toby has corns. And now I am going to
sketch," said Daphne in an authoritative tone.
"You can do your crochet: for I really suppose now
that to you and a certain class of intellects there is
a kind of pleasure to be derived from poking an

ivory hook into a loop of berlin wool and pulling it out again. But please sit so that I can't see your work, Dibb dear. The very look of that fluffy wool on this hot day almost suffocates me."

Daphne produced her drawing-block and opened her colour-box, and settled herself in a half-recumbent position on the great granite slab, and surveyed the wide landscape below her with that gaze of calm patronage which the amateur artist bestows on grand, illimitable, untranslatable Nature. She looked across the vast valley, with its silver streak of river and its distant spires, its ever varying lights and shadows—a scene which Turner would have contemplated with awe and a sense of comparative impotence; but which ignorance, as personified by Daphne, surveyed complacently, wondering where she should begin.

"I think it will make a pretty picture," she said, "if I can succeed with it."

"Why don't you do a tree, or a cottage, or something, as the drawing-master said we ought to do—just one simple little thing that one could draw correctly?" asked Martha, who was provokingly well furnished with the aggravating quality of commonsense.

"Drawing-masters are such grovellers," said Daphne, dashing in a faint outline with her facile pencil. "I would rather go on making splendid failures all my life than creep along the dull path of mediocre merit by the lines and rules of a drawing-master. I have no doubt this is going to be a splendid failure, and I shall do a devil's dance upon it presently, as Müller used in the woods near Bristol, when he couldn't please himself. But it amuses one for the moment," concluded Daphne, with whom life was all in the present, and self the centre of the universe.

She splashed away at her sky with her biggest brush, sweeping across from left to right with a wash of cobalt, and then began to edge off the colour into ragged little clouds as the despised drawing-master had taught her. There was not a cloud in the hot blue sky this midsummer afternoon, and Daphne's treatment was purely conventional.

And now she began her landscape, and tried with multitudinous dabs of gray, and green, and blue, Indian red, and Italian pink, ochre, and umber, and lake, and sienna, to imitate the glory of a fertile valley basking in the sun.

The colours were beginning to get into confusion. The foreground and the distance were all on one plane, and Daphne was on the point of flinging her block on the red sandy ground, and indulging in the luxury of a demon-dance upon her unsuccessful effort, when a voice behind her murmured quietly: "Give your background a wash of light gray, and fetch up your middle-distance with a little body colour."

"Thanks awfully," replied Daphne without looking round, and without the faintest indication of surprise. Painters in the forest were almost as common as gadflies. They seemed indigenous to the soil. "Shall I make my pine-trunks umber or Venetian red?"

"Neither," answered the unseen adviser. "Those tall pine-stems are madder-brown, except where the shadows tint them with purple."

"You are exceedingly kind," said Daphne, stifling a yawn, "but I don't think I'll go on with it. I am so obviously in a mess; I suppose nobody but a Turner ought to attempt such a valley as that."

"Perhaps not. Linnell or Vicat Cole might be able to give a faint idea of it."

"Linnell!" exclaimed Daphne. "I thought he painted nothing but wheat-fields, and that his only idea of Nature was a blaze of yellow."

"Have you seen many of his pictures?"

"One. I was taken to the Academy last year."

"Were you very pleased with what you saw?"

"Delighted—with the gowns and bonnets. It was a Saturday afternoon in the height of the season, and I plead guilty to seeing very little of the pictures. There were always people in the way, and the people were ever so much more interesting than the paintings."

"What picture can compare with a well-made gown or the latest invention in bonnets?" exclaimed the unknown with good-humoured irony.

Daphne hacked the spoiled sheet off her block with a dainty little penknife, and looked at the daub longingly, wishing that the stranger would depart and leave her free to execute a *pas seul* upon her abortive effort. But the stranger seemed to have no idea of departure. He had evidently settled himself behind her, on a camp-stool, or a rock, or some kind of seat; and he meant to stay.

She had not yet seen his face. She liked his voice, which was of the baritone order, full, and round, and grave, and his intonation was that of a man who had lived in what the world calls Society. It might not be the best possible intonation—since orators and great preachers and successful actors have another style—but it was the tone approved by the best people, and the only tone that Daphne liked.

"A drawing-master, no doubt," she thought, "whose manners have been formed in decent society."

She wiped her brushes and shut her colour-box, with languid deliberation, not yet feeling curious enough to turn and inspect the stranger, although Martha Dibb was staring at him open-mouthed, as still as a stone, and the image of astonishment. Daphne augured from that gaping mouth of

Martha's that the unknown must be somewhat eccentric in appearance or attire, and began to feel faintly inquisitive.

She rose from her recumbent attitude on the rock, drew herself as straight as an arrow, shook out her indigo-coloured serge petticoat, from beneath whose hem flashed a pair of scarlet stockings and neat buckled shoes, shook loose her mane of golden-bright hair, and looked deliberately round at Nature generally—the woods, the rocks, the brigand's cave yonder, and the stalls where toys and trifles in carved wood were set out to tempt the tourist—and finally at the stranger. He lounged at his ease on a neighbouring rock, looking up at her with a provokingly self-assured expression. Her supposition had been correct, she told herself. He evidently belonged to the artistic classes—a drawing-master, or a third-rate water-colour painter —a man whose little bits of landscape or foreign architecture would be hung near the floor, and priced at a few guineas in the official list. He was a Bohemian to the tips of his nails. He wore an old velveteen coat—Daphne was not experienced enough to know that it had been cut by a genius among tailors—a shabby felt hat lay on the grass beside him; every one of his garments had seen good service, even to the boots, whose neat shape indicated a refinement that struggled against adverse circumstances. He was young, tall, and slim, with long slender fingers, and hands that looked artistic without looking effeminate. He had dark brown hair cut close to a well-shaped head, a dark brown moustache shading a sensitive and somewhat melancholy mouth. His complexion was pale, inclining to sallowness, his nose well formed, his forehead broad and low. His eyes were of so peculiar a colour that Daphne was at first sorely perplexed as to whether they were brown or blue, and finally came to the conclusion that they were neither colour, but a variable greenish-gray. But whatever their hue she was fain to admit to herself that the eyes were handsome eyes—far too good for the man's position. Something of their beauty was doubtless owing to the thick dark lashes, the strongly marked brows. Just now the eyes, after a brief upward glance at Daphne, who fairly merited a longer regard, were fixed dreamily on the soft dreamlike landscape—the sun-steeped valley, the purple distance. It was a day for languorous dreaming; a day in which the world-worn soul might slip off the fetters of reality and roam at large in shadowland.

"Dibb," said Daphne, ever so slightly piqued at the unknown's absent air, "don't you think we ought to be going home? Poor dear Miss Toby will be anxious."

"Not before six o'clock," replied the matter-of-fact Martha. "You told her with your own lips that she wasn't to expect us before six. And what was the good of our carrying that heavy basket if we are not to eat our dinner here?"

"You have brought your dinner!" exclaimed the stranger, suddenly waking from his dream. "How very delightful! Let us improvise a picnic."

"The poor thing is hungry," thought Daphne, rather disappointed at what she considered a low trait in his character.

Martha, with her face addressed to Daphne,

began to distort her countenance in the most frightful manner, mutely protesting against the impropriety of sharing their meal with an unknown wanderer. Daphne, who was as mischievous as Robin Goodfellow, and doated on everything that was wrong, laughed these dumb appeals to scorn.

"The poor thing shall be fed," she said to herself. "Perhaps he has hardly a penny in his pockets. It will be a pleasure to give him a good meal and send him on his way rejoicing. I shall feel as meritorious as the Good Samaritan."

"Is this the basket?" asked the painter, pouncing upon the beehive receptacle which Martha had been hugging for the last five minutes. "Do let me be useful. I have a genius for picnics."

"I never heard of such impertinence!" ejaculated Miss Dibb inwardly; and then she began to wonder whether the valuable watch and chain which her father had given her on her last birthday were safe in such company, or whether her earrings might not be suddenly wrenched out of her ears.

And there was that reckless Daphne, who had

not the faintest notion of propriety, entering into the thing eagerly as a capital joke, and making herself as much at home with the nameless intruder as if she had known him all her life.

Miss Dibb had been Daphne's devoted slave for the last two years, had admired her and believed in her, and fetched and carried for her, and had been landed in all manner of scrapes and difficulties by her without a murmur; but she had never been so near revolt as at this moment, when her deep-rooted, thoroughly British sense of propriety was outraged as it had never in all Daphne's escapades been outraged before. A strange man, fairly well-mannered it is true, but shabbily clad, was to be allowed to hob and nob in a place of public resort with two of Madame Tolmache's young ladies.

Martha looked despairingly round, as if to see that help was nigh. They were not alone in the forest. This hill side at the top of the rocky walk was a favourite resort. There were stalls for toys and stalls for refreshments close at hand. There were half-a-dozen groups of idle people enjoying themselves under the tall pines and in the shadow of the big blue-gray rocks. The mother of one estimable family had taken off her boots, and was lying at full length, with her stockings exposed to the libertine gaze of passers-by. Some were eating, some were sleeping. Children with cropped heads, short petticoats, and a great deal of stocking, were flying gaudy-coloured air-balls, and screaming at each other as only French children can scream. There was not the stillness of a dense primeval wood, the awful solitude of the Great Dismal Swamp. The place was rather like a bit of Greenwich Park or Hampstead Heath on a comparatively quiet afternoon in the middle of the week.

Miss Dibb took heart of grace, and decided that her watch and earrings were safe. It was only her character that was likely to suffer. Daphne was dancing about among the rocks all this time, spreading a damask napkin on a smooth slab of granite, and making the most of the dinner. Her red stockings flashed to and fro like fireflies. She had a scarlet ribbon round her neck, and the dark serge gown was laced up the back with a scarlet cord, and, with her feathery hair flying loose and glittering in the sun, she was as bright a figure as ever lit up the foreground of a forest scene.

The unknown forgot to be useful, and sat on his granite bench lazily contemplating her as she completed her preparations.

" What an idle person you are ! " she exclaimed, looking up from her task. " Tumbler ! "

He explored the basket and produced the required article.

"Thanks. Corkscrew ! Don't run away with the idea that you are going to have wine. The corkscrew is for our lemonade."

" You needn't put such a selfish emphasis on the possessive pronoun," said the stranger. " I mean to have some of that lemonade."

Daphne surveyed the banquet critically, with her head on one side. It was not a stupendous meal for two hungry school-girls and an unknown pedestrian, whom Daphne supposed to have been on short commons for the last week or two. There was half a roasted fowl—a fowl who in his zenith had no claim to be considered a fine specimen, and who seemed to have fallen upon evil days before he was sacrificed, so gaunt was his leg, so shrunken his wing, so withered **his** breast ; there were some thin slices of carmine ham, with a bread-crumby edge instead of fat. Of one thing there was abundance, and that was the staff of life. Two long brown loaves—the genuine *pain bourgeois*—suggested a homely kind of plenty. For dessert there was a basket of wood-strawberries, a thin **slab of** Gruyère, and some small specimens of high-art confectionery, more attractive to the eye than the palate.

"Now, Dibb dear ; grace, if you please," commanded Daphne, with a mischievous side-glance at the unknown.

That French grace of poor Martha's **was a** performance which always delighted Daphne, and she wanted the wayfarer to enjoy himself. The " ongs " and " dongs " were worth hearing. Gravely the submissive Martha complied, and with solemn countenance asked a blessing on the meal.

"You can have all the fowl," said Daphne to **her guest ;** "Martha **and I** like bread and cheese ever so much better."

She tore **one** of the **big** brown loaves in two,

tossed one half to Martha, and broke a great knob
off the other for her own eating, attacking it
ravenously with her strong white teeth.

"You are more than good," replied the stranger
with his pleasantly listless air, as if there were
nothing in life worth being energetic about; "you
are actually self-sacrificing. But, to tell you the
honest truth, I have not the slightest appetite. I
had my second breakfast at one o'clock, and I had
much rather carve that elderly member of the
feathered tribe for you than eat him. I wish he
were better worthy of your consideration."

Daphne looked at him doubtfully, unconvinced.

"I know you're disparaging the bird out of
kindness to us," she said; "you might just as well
eat a good luncheon. Martha and I adore bread
and cheese."

She emphasised this assertion with a stealthy
frown at poor Miss Dibb, who saw her dinner thus
coolly confiscated for the good of a suspicious-
looking interloper.

"You doat upon Gruyère, don't you, Martha?"
she demanded.

"I like it pretty well," answered Miss Dibb sulkily; "but I think the holes are the nicest part."

The stranger was cutting up the meagre fowl, giving the wing and breast to Daphne, the sinewy leg to Martha, who was the kind of girl to go through life getting the legs of fowls and the back seats in opera-boxes, and the worst partners at afternoon dances.

Finding the unknown inflexible, and being herself desperately hungry, Daphne ended by taking her share of the poultry, while her guest ate a few strawberries and munched a crust of bread, lying along the grass all the while, almost at her feet. It was a new experience, and the more horrified Martha looked the more Daphne enjoyed it.

What was life to her but the present hour, with its radiant sun and glad earth flushed with colour, the scent of the pines, the hum of the bees, the delight of the butterflies flashing across the blue? Utterly innocent in her utter ignorance of evil, she saw no snare in such simple joys, she had no premonition of danger. Her worst suspicion of the

stranger was that he might be poor. That was
the only social crime whereof she knew. And the
more convinced she felt of his poverty, the more
determined she was to be civil to him.

He lay at her feet, on a carpet of fir-needles,
looking up at her with an admiration almost as
purely artistic as that which he had felt an hour ago
for a green and purple lizard which he had caught
asleep on one of the rocks, and which had darted
up a sheer wall of granite, swift as a sun-ray, at
the light touch of his finger-tip. With a love of
the beautiful almost as abstract as that which he
had felt for the graceful curves and rainbow tints of
the lizard, he lay and basked in the light of this
school-girl's violet eyes, and watched the play of
sunbeam and shadow on her golden hair. To him,
too, the present hour was all in all—an hour of sunlight and perfume and balmiest atmosphere, an
hour's sweet idleness, empty of thought and care.

The face he looked at was not one of those
perfect faces which would bear to be transfixed in
marble. It was a countenance whose chief beauty
lay in colour and expression—a face full of variety;

now whimsically gay, now pouting, now pert; anon suddenly pensive. Infinitely bewitching in some phases, it was infinitely provoking in others: but, under all conditions, it was a face full of interest.

The complexion was brilliant, the true English red and white: no ivory-pale beauty this, with the sickly tints of Gibson's painted Venus, but the creamy fairness and the vivid rose of health, and youth, and happiness. The eyes were of darkest gray, that deep violet which, under thick dark lashes, looks black as night. The nose was short and *retroussé*, nothing to boast of in noses; the mouth was a trifle wide, but the lips were of loveliest form and richest carmine, the teeth flashing beneath them absolutely perfect. Above those violet eyes arched strongly-marked brows of darkest brown, contrasting curiously with the thick fringe of golden hair. Altogether the face was more original in its beauty than any which the stranger had looked upon for a long time.

"Have you any sketches to show us?" asked Daphne when she had finished her dinner.

"No; I have not been sketching this morning

and if I had done anything I doubt if it would have been worth looking at. You must not suppose I am a grand artist. But if you don't mind lending me your block and your colour-box for half an hour I should like to make a little sketch now."

"Cool," thought Daphne. "But calm impudence is this gentleman's leading characteristic."

She handed him block and box with an amused smile.

"Are you going to paint the valley?" she asked.

"No; I leave that for a new Turner. I am only going to try my hand at a rock with a young lady sitting on it."

"I'm sure Martha won't mind being painted," replied Daphne, with a mischievous glance at Miss Dibb, who was sitting bolt upright on her particular block of granite, the image of stiffness and dumb disapproval. She was a thick-set girl with sandy hair and freckles, not bad-looking after her homely fashion, but utterly wanting in grace.

"I couldn't think of taking such a liberty with Miss Martha," returned the stranger; "the freemasonry of art puts me at my ease with you. Would you mind sitting quiet for half an hour or so. That semi-recumbent position will do beautifully."

He sketched in rock and figure as he spoke, with a free facile touch that showed a practised hand.

"I'm sure you can paint beautifully," said Daphne, watching his pencil as he sat a little way off, glancing up at her every now and then.

"Wait till you see how I shall interpret your lilies and roses. I ought to be as good a colourist as Rubens or John Phillip to do you justice."

She had fallen into a reposeful attitude after finishing her meal, her arms folded on the rock, her head resting on the folded arms, her eyes gazing sleepily at the sunlit valley in front of her, one little foot pendent from the edge of the greenish gray stone, the other tucked under her dark blue skirt, a mass of yellow tresses falling over one dark blue shoulder, and a scarlet ribbon fluttering on the other.

Martha Dibb looked more and more horrified. Could there be a lower deep than this? To sit for one's portrait to an unknown artist in a shabby coat. The man was unquestionably a vagabond, although he did not make havoc of his aspirates like poor dear papa; and Daphne was bringing disgrace on Madame Tolmache's whole establishment.

"Suppose I should meet him in Regent Street one day after I leave school, and he were to speak to me, what would mamma and Jane say?" thought Miss Dibb.

CHAPTER II.

DAPHNE was as still as a statue, her vanity gratified by this homage to her charms. There had been nobody to admire her at Asnières but the old music-master, into whose hat she had sometimes put a little bouquet from the trim suburban garden, or a spray of acacia from the grove that screened the maiden meditations of Madame Tolmache's pupils from the vulgar gaze of the outside world. She retained her recumbent attitude patiently for nearly an hour, half-asleep in the balmy afternoon atmosphere, while the outraged Martha sat on her rock apart, digging her everlasting crochet-hook into the fluffy mass of wool, and saying never a word.

The stranger was nearly as silent as Martha. He was working industriously at his sketch, and smoking his cigar as he worked, having first ascertained that the ladies were tolerant of the weed. He painted in a large dashing style that got over the ground very quickly, and made a good effect. He had nearly finished his sketch of the figure on the rock—the indigo gown, scarlet ribbon, bright hair, and dark luminous eyes, when Daphne jumped up suddenly, and vowed that her every limb was an agony to her.

"I couldn't endure it an instant longer!" she exclaimed. "I hope you've finished."

"Not quite; but you may change your attitude as much as you like if you'll only keep your head the same way. I am working at the face now."

"What are you going to do with the picture when it's finished?"

"Keep it till my dying day."

"I thought you would perhaps give it—I

mean sell it—to me. I could not afford a large price, for my people are very poor, but——"

"Your looking-glass will show you a better portrait than this poor sketch of mine. And, in after years, even this libellous daub will serve to remind me of a happy hour in my life."

"I am glad you have enjoyed yourself," said Daphne; "but I really wish you had eaten that fowl. Have you far to go home to dinner?"

"Only to Fontainebleau."

"You are living there?"

"I am staying there. I may strike my tent and be across the Jura to-morrow night. I never live anywhere."

"But haven't you a home and people?"

"I have a kind of home, but no people."

"Poor fellow!" murmured Daphne, with exquisite compassion. "Are you an orphan?"

"Yes; my father died nine years ago, my mother last year."

"How awfully sad! No brothers or sisters?"

"None. I am a crystallisation, the last of a vanishing race. And now I have done as much as I dare to your portrait. Any attempt at finish would result in failure. I am writing the place and the date in the corner of my sketch. May I write your name?"

"My name!" exclaimed Daphne, her eyes sparkling with mischief, her cheeks curving into dimples.

"Yes; your name. You have a name, I suppose: unless you are the nameless spirit of sunlit woodlands, masquerading in a blue gown?"

"My name—is—Poppæa," faltered Daphne, whose latest chapter of Roman history had been the story of Nero and his various crimes, toned down and expurgated to suit young ladies' schools.

Poppæa Sabina, thus chastely handled, had appeared nothing worse than a dressy lady of extravagant tastes, who took elaborate care of her complexion, and had a fancy for shoeing her mules with gold.

"Did you say Poppet?" inquired the stranger.

"No; Poppæa. You must have heard the name before, I should think. It is a Roman name. My father is a great classical scholar, and he chose it for me. And pray what is your name ?"

" Nero."

The stranger pronounced the word without moving a muscle of his face, still intent upon his sketch; for it is vain for a man to say he has finished a thing of that kind; so long as his brushes are within reach, he will be putting in new touches. There was not a twinkle in those dubious eyes of his—not an upward move of those mobile lips. He was as grave as a judge.

" I don't believe it !" cried Daphne, bouncing up from her rock.

" Don't believe what ? "

" That your name is Nero."

" Why not ? Have I not as good a right to bear a Roman name as you have ? Suppose I had a classical father as well as you. Why not ? "

" It is too absurd."

" Many things are absurd which yet are absolutely true."

" And you are really called Nero ? "

" As really as you are called Poppæa."

"It is so dreadfully like a dog's name."

"It is a dog's name. But you may call your dog Bill, or Joe, or Paul, or Peter. I don't think that makes any difference. I would sooner have some dogs for my namesakes than some men."

"Dibb, dear," said Daphne, turning sharply upon the victim of her folly, the long-suffering, patient Martha. "What's the time?"

She had a watch of her own, a neat little gold hunter; but it was rarely in going order for two consecutive days, and she was generally dependent on the methodical Dibb for all information as to the flight of time.

"A quarter to five."

"Then we must be going home instantly. How could you let me stay so long, you foolish girl? I am sure it must be more than an hour's walk to the town, and we promised poor dear Toby to be home by six."

"It isn't my fault," remarked Miss Dibb; "I should have been glad to go ever so long ago, if you had thought fit."

"Hurry up, then, Dibb dear. Put away your

crochet. Have you quite done with my block?" to the unknown. "Thank you muchly. And now my box? Those go into the basket. Thanks, awfully," as he helped her to pack the tumblers, corkscrew, plates, and knives, which had served for their primitive repast. "And now we will wish you good-day—Mr.—Nero."

"On no account. I am going to carry that basket back to Fontainebleau for you."

"All along that dusty high road. We couldn't think of such a thing; could we, Martha?"

"I don't know that my opinion is of much account," said Martha stiffly.

"Don't, you dear creature!" cried Daphne, darting at her, and hugging her affectionately. "Don't try to be ill-tempered, for you can't do it. The thing is an ignominious failure. You were created to be good-natured, and nice, and devoted—especially to me."

"You know how fond I am of you," murmured Martha reproachfully; "and you take a mean advantage of me when you go on so."

"How am I going on? Is it very dreadful

to let a gentleman carry a heavy basket for
me ?"

"A gentleman!" muttered Martha, with a
supercilious glance at the stranger's well-worn
velveteen.

He was standing a little way off, out of hearing,
taking a last long look at the valley.

"Yes; and every inch a gentleman, though
his coat is shabby, and though he may be as poor
as Job, and though he makes game of me!"
protested Daphne with conviction.

"Have your own way," replied Martha.

"I generally do," answered Daphne.

And so they went slowly winding downhill in
the westering sunshine, all among the gray rocks
on which the purple shadows were deepening,
the warm umber lights glowing, while the rosy
evening light came creeping up in the distant
west, and the voice of an occasional bird, so
rare in this Gallic wood, took a vesper sound
in the summer stillness.

The holiday makers had all gone home. The
French matron who had taken her rest so luxuriously,

surrounded by her olive-branches, had put on her boots and departed. The women who sold cakes and fruit, and wooden paper-knives, had packed up their wares and gone away. All was silence and loneliness; and for a little while Daphne and her companions wandered on in quiet enjoyment of the scene and the atmosphere, treading the mossy, sandy path that wound in and out among the big rocks, sometimes nearly losing themselves, and anon following the blue arrow-points which a careful hand had painted on the rocks to show them which way they should go.

But Daphne was not given to silence. She found something to talk about before they had gone very far.

"You have travelled immensely, I suppose?" she said to the stranger.

"I don't know exactly what significance you attach to the word. Young ladies use such large words nowadays for such very small things. From a scientific explorer's point of view, my wanderings have been very limited, but I daresay one of Cook's tourists would consider me a respectable traveller.

I have never seen the buried cities of Central America, nor surveyed the world from the top of Mount Everest, nor even climbed the Caucasus, nor wandered by stormy Hydaspes; but I have done Egypt, and Algeria, and Greece, and all that is tolerably worth seeing in Southern Europe, and have tried my hand, or rather my legs, at Alpine climbing, and have come to the conclusion that, although Nature is mountainous, life is every-where more or less flat, stale, and unprofitable."

"I'm sure I shouldn't feel that if I were free to roam the world, and could paint as sweetly as you do."

"I had a sweet subject, remember."

"Please don't," cried Daphne; "I rather like you when you are rude, but if you flatter I shall hate you."

"Then I'll be rude. To win your liking I would be more uncivil than Petruchio."

"Katharine was a fool!" exclaimed Daphne, skipping up the craggy side of one of the biggest rocks. "I have always despised her. To begin so well, and end so tamely."

"If you don't take care you'll end by slipping

off that rock, and spraining an ankle or two," said
Nero warningly.

"Not I," answered Daphne confidently; "you
don't know how used I am to climbing. Oh, look
at that too delicious lizard!"

She was on her knees admiring the emerald-
hued changeful creature. She touched it only with
her breath, and it flashed away from her and
vanished in some crevice of the rock.

"Silly thing, did it think I wanted to hurt it,
when I was only worshipping its beauty?" she cried.

Then she rose suddenly, and stood on the rock,
a slim girlish figure, with fluttering drapery, poised
as lightly as Mercury, gazing round her, admiring
the tall slim stems of the beeches growing in
groups like clustered columns, the long vista of
rocks, the dark wall of fir-trees, mounting up and
up to the edge of a saffron-tinted sky—for these
loiterers had lost count of time since steady-going
Martha looked at her reliable watch, and the last
of the finches had sung his lullaby to his wife and
family, and the golden ship called Sol had gone
down to Night's dark sea.

"Come down, you absurd creature!" exclaimed Nero, with a peremptory voice, winding one arm about the light figure, and lifting the girl off the rock as easily as if she had been a feather-weight.

"You are very horrid!" protested Daphne indignantly. "You are ever so much ruder than Petruchio. Why shouldn't I stand on that rock? I was only admiring the landscape!"

"No doubt, and two minutes hence you would be calling upon us to admire a fine example of a sprained ankle."

"I'm sure if your namesake was ever as unkind to my namesake, it's no wonder she died young," said Daphne, pouting.

"I believe he was occasionally a little rough upon her," answered the artist with his imperturbable air. "But of course you have read your Tacitus and your Suetonius in the original. Young ladies know everything nowadays."

"The Roman history we read is by a clergyman, written expressly for ladies' schools," said Miss Dibb demurely.

"How intensely graphic and interesting that chronicle must be!" retorted the stranger.

They had come to the end of the winding path among the rocks by this time, and were in a long, straight road, cut through the heart of the forest, between tall trees that seemed to have outgrown their strength—weedy-looking trees, planted too thickly, and only able to push their feeble growth up towards the sun, with no room for spreading boughs or interlacing roots. The evening light was growing grave and gray. Bats were skimming across the path, uncomfortably near Daphne's flowing hair. Miss Dibb began to grumble.

"How dreadfully we have loitered!" she cried, looking at her watch. "It is nearly eight, and we have so far to go. What will Miss Toby say?"

"Well, she will moan a little, no doubt," answered Daphne lightly, "and will tell us that her heart has been in her mouth for the last hour, which need not distress us much, as we know it's a physical impossibility; and that anyone might knock her down with a feather—another obvious impossibility, seeing that poor Toby weighs eleven stone—and then I shall kiss her and make much of her, and give her the packet of nougat I mean to buy on the way home, and all will be sunshine. She takes a sticky delight in nougat. And now please talk and amuse us," said Daphne, turning to the artist with an authoritative air. "Tell us about some of your travels, or tell us where you live when you're at home."

"I think I'd rather talk of my travels. I've just come from Italy."

"Where you have been painting prodigiously, of course. It is a land of pictures, is it not?"

"Yes; but Nature's pictures are even better than the treasures of art."

"If ever I should marry," said Daphne with a dreamy look, as if she were contemplating an event far off in the dimness of twenty years hence, "I should insist upon my husband taking me to Italy."

"Perhaps he wouldn't be able to afford the expense," suggested the practical Martha.

"Then I wouldn't marry him," Daphne retorted decisively.

"Isn't that rather a mercenary notion?" asked the gentleman with the basket.

"Not at all. Do you suppose I should marry just for the sake of having a husband? If ever I do marry—which I think is more than doubtful—it will be, first and foremost, in order that I may do everything I wish to do, and have everything I want to have. Is there anything singular in that?"

"No; I suppose it is a young beauty's innate idea of marriage. She sees herself in her glass, and recognises perfection, and knows her own value."

"Are you married?" asked Daphne abruptly, eager to change the conversation when the stranger became complimentary.

"No."

"Engaged?"

"Yes."

"What is she like?" inquired Daphne eagerly. "Please tell us about her. It will be ever so much more interesting than Italy; for, after all, when one hasn't seen a country description goes for so little. What is she like?"

"I could best answer that question in one word if I were to say she is perfection."

"You called me perfection just now," said Daphne pettishly.

"I was talking of your face. She is perfection in all things. Perfectly pure, and true, and good, and noble. She is handsome, highly accomplished, rich."

"And yet you go wandering about the world in that coat," exclaimed Daphne, too impulsive to be polite.

"It is shabby, is it not? But if you knew how comfortable it is you wouldn't wonder that I have an affection for it."

"Go on about the young lady, please. Have you been long engaged to her?"

"Ever since I can remember, in my heart of hearts: she was my bright particular star when I was a boy at school: she was my sole incentive to work, or decent behaviour, when I was at the University. And now I am not going to say any more about her. I think I have told you enough to gratify any reasonable curiosity. Ask me conundrums, young ladies, if you please, or do something to amuse me. Remember, I am carrying the basket, and a man is something more than a beast of burden. My mind requires relaxation."

Martha Dibb grinned all over her broad frank face. Riddles were her delight. She had little manuscript books filled with them in her scrawly, pointed writing. She began at once, like a musical-box that has been wound up, and did not leave off asking conundrums **till** they were half-way down the long street leading to the palace, near which Miss Toby and her pupils had their lodging.

But Daphne had no intention that the stranger should learn exactly where she lived. Reckless as she was, mirthful and mischievous as Puck or Robin Goodfellow, she had still a dim idea that her conduct was not exactly correct, or would not be correct **in England**. On the Continent, of course, there must be a certain license. English travellers dined at public tables, and gamed in public rooms —were altogether more sociable and open to approach than on their native soil. It was only a chosen few—the peculiarly gifted in stiffness—who

retained their glacial crust through every change of
scene and climate, and who would perish rather
than cross the street ungloved, or discourse
familiarly with an unaccredited stranger. But,
even with due allowance for Continental laxity,
Daphne felt that she had gone a little too far. So
she pulled up suddenly at the corner of a side street,
and demanded her basket.

"What does that mean?" asked the painter
with a look of lazy surprise.

"Only that this is our way home, and that we
won't trouble you to carry the basket any further,
thanks intensely."

"But I am going to carry it to your door."

"It's awfully good of you to propose it, but our
governess would be angry with us for imposing on
the kindness of a stranger, and I am afraid we
should get into trouble."

"Then I haven't a word to say," answered the
painter, smiling at her blushing eloquent face.
Verily a speaking face—beautiful just as a sunlit
meadow is beautiful, because of the lights and
shadows that flit and play perpetually across it.

"Do you live in this street?" he asked.

"No; our house is in the second turning to the right, seven doors from the corner," said Daphne, who had obtained possession of the basket. "Good-bye."

She ran off with light swift foot, followed lumpishly and breathlessly by the scandalised Martha.

"Daphne, how could you tell him such an outrageous story?" she exclaimed.

"Do you think I was going to tell him the truth?" asked Daphne, still fluttering on, light as a lapwing. "We should have had him calling on Miss Toby to-morrow morning to ask if we were fatigued by our walk, or perhaps singing the serenade from Don Giovanni under our windows to-night. Now, Martha dearest, don't say one word; I know I have behaved shamefully, but it has been awful fun, hasn't it?"

"I'm sure I felt ready to sink through the ground all the time," panted Martha.

"Darling, the ground and you are both too solid for there to be any fear of that."

They had turned a corner by this time, and doubling and winding, always at a run, they came very speedily to the quiet spot near the palace, where their governess had lodged them in a low blind-looking white house, with only one window that commanded a view of the street.

They had been so fleet of foot, and had so doubled on the unknown, that, from this upper window, they had presently the satisfaction of seeing him come sauntering along the empty street, careless, indifferent, with dreamy eyes looking forward into vacancy, a man without a care.

"He doesn't look as if he minded our having given him the slip one little bit," said Daphne.

"Why should he?" asked the matter-of-fact Martha. "I daresay he was tired of carrying the basket."

"Go your ways," said Daphne with a faint sigh, waving her hand at the vanishing figure. "Go your ways over mountain and sea, through wood and valley. This world is a big place, and it isn't likely you and I will ever meet again." Then, turning to her companion with a sudden change of manner, she exclaimed: "Martha, I believe we have both made a monstrous mistake."

"As how?" asked Miss Dibb stupidly.

"In taking him for a poor artist."

"He looks like one."

"Not he. There is nothing about him but his coat that looks poor, and he wears that as if it were purple and ermine. Did you notice his eye when he ordered us to change the conversation, an eye accustomed to look at inferiors? And there is a careless pride in his manner, like a man who believes that the world was made on purpose for him, yet doesn't want to make any fuss about it. Then he is engaged to a rich lady, and he has been at a university. No, Martha, I am sure he is no wandering artist living on his pencil."

"Then he must think all the worse of us," said Martha solemnly.

"What does it matter?" asked Daphne, with a careless shrug. "We have seen the last of each other."

"You can never be sure of that. One might meet him at a party."

"I don't think you will," said Daphne, faintly supercilious, "and the chances are ever so many to one against even my meeting him anywhere."

Here Miss Toby burst into the room. She had been lying down in an adjacent chamber, resting her poor bilious head, when the girls came softly in, and had only just heard their voices.

"Oh, you dreadful girls, what hours of torture you have caused me!" she exclaimed. "I thought something must have happened."

"Something did happen," said Daphne; whereupon Martha thought she was going to confess everything.

"What?"

"A lizard."

"Did it sting you?"

"No; it darted away when I looked at it. A lovely glittering green thing. I wish I could tame one and wear it for a necklace. And I nearly fell off a rock; and I tried hard to paint the valley, and made a most dismal failure. But the view from the hill is positively delicious, Toby dear, and the rocks are wonderful; huge masses of granite tumbled about among the trees anyhow, as if Titans had been pelting one another. It's altogether lovely. You must go with us to-morrow, Toby love."

Miss Toby, diverted from her intention to scold, shook her head despondingly.

"I should like it of all things," she sighed. "But I am such a bad walker, and the heat always affects my head. Besides, I think we ought to go over the palace to-morrow. There is so much instruction to be derived from a place so full of historical associations."

"No doubt," answered the flippant Daphne, "though if you were to tell me that it had been built by Julius Cæsar or Alfred the Great, I should hardly be wise enough to contradict you."

"My dear Daphne, after you have been so carefully grounded in history," remonstrated Miss Toby.

"I know, dear; but then you see I have never built anything on the ground. It's all very well to dig out foundations, but if one never gets any further than that! But we'll see the palace to-morrow, and you shall teach me no end of history while we are looking at pictures and things."

"If my poor head be well enough," sighed Miss Toby, and then she began to move languidly to and fro, arranging for the refreshment of her pupils, who wanted their supper.

When the supper was ready, Daphne could eat nothing, although five minutes before she had declared herself ravenous. She was too excited to eat. She talked of the forest, the view, the heat, the sky, everything except the stranger, and his name was trembling on her lips perpetually. Every now and then she pulled herself up abruptly in the middle of a sentence, and flashed a vivid glance at stolid Martha, her dark gray eyes shining like stars, full of mischievous light. She would have liked to tell Miss Toby everything, but to do so might be to surrender all future liberty. Headache or no headache, the honest little governess would never have allowed her pupils to wander about alone again, could she have beheld them, in her mind's eye, picnicking with a nameless stranger.

There was a little bit of garden at the back of the low, white house, hardly more than a green courtyard, with a square grass plot and a few shrubs, into which enclosure the windows all looked, save that one peep-hole towards the street. Above the white wall that shut in the bit of green rose the foliage of a much larger garden—acacias shedding their delicate perfume on the cool night, limes just breaking into flower, dark-leaved magnolias, tulip-trees, birch and aspen—a lovely variety of verdure. And over all this shone the broad disk of a ripening moon, flooding the world with light.

When supper was over Daphne bounded out into the moonlit garden, and began to play at battledore and shuttlecock. She was all life and fire and movement, and could not have sat still for the world.

"Come," she cried to Martha; "bring your battledore. A match for a franc's worth of nougat."

Miss Dibb had settled herself to her everlasting crochet by the light of two tall candles. Miss Toby was reading a Tauchnitz novel.

"I'm tired to death," grumbled Martha. "I'm

E 2

sure we must have walked miles upon miles. How can you be so restless?"

"How can you mope indoors on such an exquisite night?" exclaimed Daphne. "I feel as if I could send my shuttlecock up to the moon. Come out and be beaten! No; you are too wise. You know that I should win to-night."

The little toy of cork and feathers quivered high up in the bright air; the slender, swaying figure bent back like a reed as the girl looked upward; the fair golden head moved with every motion of the battledore as the player bent or rose to anticipate the flying cork.

She was glad to be out there alone. She was thinking of the unknown all the time. She could not get him out of her mind. She had a vague unreasonable idea that he must be near her; that he saw her as she played; that he was hiding somewhere in the shadow yonder, peeping over the wall; that he was in the moon—in the night—everywhere; that it was his breath which fluttered those leaves trembling above the wall; that it was his footfall she heard rustling among the shrubs—a stealthy,

mysterious sound mingling with the plish-plash of
the fountain in the next garden. She had talked
lightly enough a little while ago of having seen the
last of him: yet now, alone with her thoughts in
the moonlit garden, it seemed as if this nameless
stranger were interwoven with the fabric of her life,
a part of her destiny for evermore.

CHAPTER III.

ANOTHER brilliant summer day, a cloudless blue sky, a world steeped in sunshine. On the broad gravelled space in front of the palace-railings the heat and glare would have been too much for a salamander, and even Daphne, who belonged to the salamander species in so much as she had an infinite capacity for enjoying sunshine, blinked a little as she crossed the shelterless promenade, under her big tussore parasol, a delightfully cool-looking figure in a plain white muslin gown, and a muslin shepherdess hat.

Poor Miss Toby's chronic headache had been a little worse this morning. Heroically had she

striven to fulfil her duty, albeit to lift her leaden
head from the pillow was absolute agony. She
sat at the breakfast-table, white, ghastly, uncom-
plaining, pouring out coffee, at the very odour of
which her bilious soul sickened. Vainly did
Daphne entreat her to go back to bed, and to
leave her charges to take care of themselves as
they had done yesterday.

"We won't go to the forest any more till you
are able to go with us," said Daphne, dimly conscious that her behaviour in that woodland region
had been open to blame. "We can just go quietly
to the palace, and stroll through the rooms with
the few tourists who are likely to be there to-day.
The Fontainebleau season has hardly begun, don't
you know, and we may have nobody but the guide,
and of course he must be a respectable person."

"My dear, I was sent here to take care of
you both, and I must do my duty," answered
Miss Toby with a sickly smile. "Yesterday my
temples throbbed so that I could hardly move,
but I am a little better to-day, and I shall put on
my bonnet and come with you."

She rose, staggered a few paces towards the adjacent chamber, and reeled like a landsman at sea. Then she sank into the nearest chair, and breathed a weary sigh.

"It's no use, Toby darling," cried Daphne, bending over her with tenderest sympathy. To be tender, sweet, and sympathetic in little outward ways, tones of voice, smiles, and looks, was one of Daphne's dangerous gifts. "My dearest Toby, why struggle against the inevitable?" she urged. "It is simply one of your regular bilious attacks. All you have to do is to lie quietly in a dark room and sleep it off, just as you have so often done before. To-morrow you will be as well as I am."

"Then why not wait till to-morrow for seeing the palace," said Miss Toby faintly, "and amuse yourselves at home, for once in a way? You really ought to study a little, Daphne. Madame will be horrified if she finds you have done no work all this time."

"But I do work of an evening—sometimes, dearest," expostulated Daphne; "and I'm sure you would not like us to be half suffocated all day in this stifling little salon, poring over horrid books. We should be having the **fever** next, and then how would you account to Madame for your stewardship ? "

" Don't be irreverent, Daphne," said Miss Toby, who thought that any use of scriptural phrases out of church was a kind of blasphemy. " I think you would really be better indoors upon such a day **as this; but I feel** too languid to argue the point. What would you like best, Martha ? "

Miss Dibb, who employed every odd scrap of spare time **in** the development of her *magnum opus* in crochet-work, **looked up with a** glance of indifference, and **was** about to declare her willingness to stay indoors for ever, **so** that the crochet counterpane might flourish and wax **wide, when** a stealthy frown from Daphne checked her.

"Daphne would rather **see** the palace to-day, I know," she replied meekly, "and I think," with **a** nervous glance **at her** schoolfellow, **who** was **scowling savagely,** "**I think I** would rather go too."

" Well," sighed Miss Toby, " I have made an

effort, but I feel that I could not endure the glare out of doors. You must go alone. Be sure you are both very quiet, if there are tourists about. Don't giggle, or look round at people, or make fun of their gowns and bonnets, as you are too fond of doing. It is horribly unladylike. And if any stranger should try to get into conversation with you—of course only a low-bred person would do such a thing—pray remember that your own self-respect would counsel you to be dumb."

"Can you suppose we would speak to anyone?" exclaimed Daphne, as she tripped away to her little bedroom, next door to Miss Toby's. It was the queerest little room, with a narrow, white-muslin-curtained bed in a recess, and a marvellous piece of furniture which was washstand, chest of drawers, and dressing-table all in one. A fly-spotted glass, inclining from the wall above this *multum in parvo,* was Daphne's only mirror.

Here she put on her muslin hat, with a bouquet of blue cornflowers perched coquettishly on the brim, making a patch of bright cool colour that refreshed the eye. Never had she looked prettier

than this midsummer morning. Even the fly-
spotted clouded old glass told her as much as
that.

"If—if he were to be doing the *château* to-
day," she thought, tremulous with excitement,
"how strange it would be. But that's not likely.
He is not of the common class of tourists, who
all follow the same beaten track. I daresay he
will idle away the afternoon in the woods, just
as he did yesterday."

"Martha, shall we go to the forest to-day, and
leave the *château* to be done to-morrow with Toby,"
Daphne asked, when she and her companion were
crossing the wide parade-ground, where the soldiers
trotted by with a great noise and clatter early in
the morning, with a fanfare of trumpets and an
occasional roll of a drum. "It might seem kinder
to poor dear Toby, don't you know."

"I think it would be very wrong, Daphne,"
answered the serious Martha. "We told Miss
Toby we were going to the palace, and we are
bound to go straight there and nowhere else.
Besides, I want to see the pictures and statues

and things, and I am sick to death of that forest."

"After one day! Oh, Martha, what an unromantic soul you must have. I could live and die there, if I had pleasant company. I have always envied Rosalind and Celia."

"They must have been very glad when they got home," said Martha.

Out of the blinding whiteness of the open street they went in at a gate to a gravelled quadrangle, where the sun seemed to burn with yet more fiery heat. Even Daphne felt breathless, but it was a pleasant feeling, the delight of absolute summer, which comes so seldom in the changeful year. Then they went under an archway, and into the inner quadrangle, with the white palace on all sides of them. It wanted some minutes of eleven, and they were shown into a cool official-looking room, where they were to wait till the striking of the hour. The room was panelled, painted white, a room of Louis the Fourteenth's time most likely; what little furniture there was being quaint and rococo, but not old. The blinds were down, the shutters half-closed, and the room was in deep shadow.

"How nice!" gasped Martha, who had been panting like a fish out of water all the way.

"It is like coming into a grotto," said Daphne, sinking into a chair.

"It is not half so nice as the forest," said a voice in the semi-darkness.

Daphne gave a visible start. She had mused upon the possibility of meeting her acquaintance of yesterday, and had decided that the thing was unlikely. Yet her spirits had been buoyed by a lurking idea that he might crop up somehow before the day was done. But to find him here at the very beginning of things was startling.

"Did you know that we were coming here to-day?" she faltered.

"Hadn't the slightest idea; but I wanted to see the place myself," he answered coolly.

Daphne blushed rosy-red, deeply ashamed of her foolish, impulsive speech. The stranger had been sitting in that cool shade for the last ten minutes, and his eyes had grown accustomed to the obscurity. He saw the blush, he saw the bright expressive face under the muslin hat, the slim figure in the white frock, every line sharply accentuated against a gray background, the slender hand in a long Swedish glove. She looked more womanly in her white gown and hat—and yet more childlike—than she had looked yesterday in blue and scarlet.

They sat for about five minutes in profound silence. Daphne, usually loquacious, felt as if she could not have spoken for the world. Martha was by nature stolid and inclined to dumbness. The stranger was watching Daphne's face in a lazy reverie, thinking that his hurried sketch of yesterday was not half so lovely as the original, and yet it had seemed to him almost the prettiest head he had ever painted.

" The provoking minx has hardly one good feature," he thought. " It is an utterly unpaintable beauty—a beauty of colour, life, and movement. Photograph her asleep, and she would be as plain as a pike-staff. How different from——"

He gave a faint sigh, and was startled from his

musing by the door opening with a bang and an official calling out, " This way, ladies and gentlemen."

They crossed the blazing court-yard in the wake of a brisk little gentleman in uniform, who led them up a flight of stone steps, and into a stony hall. Thence to the chapel, and then to an upper storey, **and** over polished floors through long suites of rooms, everyone made more **or** less sacred by historical memories. Here was the table on which Napoleon the Great signed his abdication, while his Old Guard waited in the quadrangle below. **Daphne** looked first at the table and then out of the window, almost as if she expected to see that faithful soldiery drawn up in the stony court-yard—grim bearded men who had fought and conquered on so many a field, **victors of Lodi and** Arcola, Austerlitz and Jena, Friedland and Wagram, and who knew now that all was over and their leader's star had gone down.

Then to rooms hallowed by noble Marie Antoinette, lovely alike in felicity and in ruin. Smaller, prettier, more homelike rooms came next, where the Citizen King and his gentle wife tasted the **sweetness of** calm domestic joys; a tranquil gracious

family circle; to be transferred, with but a brief
interval of stormy weather, to the quiet reaches of
the Thames, in Horace Walpole's beloved "County
of Twits." Then back to the age of tournaments
and tented fields; and, lo! they were in the rooms
which courtly Francis built and adorned, and
glorified by his august presence. Here, amidst
glitter of gold and glow of colour, the great king—
Charles the Fifth's rival and victor—lived and loved,
and shed sunshine upon an adoring court. Here
from many a canvas, fresh as if painted yesterday,
look the faces of the past. Names fraught with
romantic memories sanctify every nook and corner
of the palace. Everywhere appears the cypher of
Diana of Poitiers linked with that of her royal lover,
Henry the Second. Catherine de Médicis must have
looked upon those interlaced initials many a time in
the period of her probation, looked, and held her
peace, and schooled herself to patience, waiting till
Fortune's wheel should turn and bring her day of
power. Here in this long, lofty chamber, sunlit,
beautiful, the fated Monaldeschi's life-blood stained
the polished floor.

"To say the least of it, the act was an impertinence on Queen Christina's part, seeing that she was only a visitor at Fontainebleau," said the stranger languidly. " Don't you think so, Poppæa ? "

Daphne required to have the whole story told her; that particular event not having impressed itself on her mind.

" I have read all through Bonnechose's history of France, and half way from the beginning again," she explained. " But when one sits droning history in a row of droning girls, even a murder doesn't make much impression upon one. It's all put in the same dull, dry way. This year there was a great scarcity of corn. The poor in the provinces suffered extreme privations. Queen Christina, of Sweden, while on a visit at Fontainebleau, ordered the execution of her counsellor Monaldeschi. There was also a plague at Marseilles. The Dauphin died suddenly in the fifteenth year of his age. The king held a Bed of Justice for the first time since he ascended the throne. That is the kind of thing, you know."

" I can conceive that so bald a calendar would

scarcely take a firm grip upon one's memory," assented the stranger. "Details are apt to impress the mind more than events."

After this came the rooms which the Pope occupied during his captivity—rooms that had double and treble memories; here a nuptial-chamber, there a room all a-glitter with gilding—a room that had sheltered Charles the Fifth, and afterwards fair, and not altogether fortunate, Anne of Austria. Daphne felt as if her brain would hardly hold so much history. She felt a kind of relief when they came to a theatre, where plays had been acted before Napoleon the Third and his lovely empress in days that seemed to belong to her own life.

"I think I was born then," she said naïvely.

There had been no other visitors—no tourists of high or low degree. The two girls and the unknown had had the palace to themselves, and the guide, mollified by a five-franc piece slipped into his hand by the gentleman, had allowed them to make their circuit at a somewhat more leisurely pace than that brisk trot on which he usually insisted.

Yet for all this it was still early when they came

down the double flight of steps and found themselves once again in the quadrangle, the Court of Farewells, so called from the day when the great emperor bade adieu to pomp and power, and passed like a splendid apparition from the scene he had glorified. The sun had lost none of his fervour—nay, had ascended to his topmost heaven, and was pouring down his rays upon the baking earth.

"Let us go to the gardens and feed the carp," said Nero, and it was an infinite relief, were it only for the refreshment of the eye, to find themselves under green leaves and by the margin of a lovely lake, statues of white marble gleaming yonder at the end of verdant arcades, fountains plashing. Here under the trees a delicious coolness and stillness contrasted with the glare of light on the open space yonder, where an old woman sat at a stall, set out with cakes and sweetmeats, ready to supply food for the carp-feeders.

"Yes: let us feed the carp," cried Daphne, running out into this sunlit space, her white gown looking like some saintly raiment in the supernatural light of a transfiguration. "That will be lovely!

I have heard of them. They are intensely old, are they not—older than the palace itself?"

"They are said to have been here when Henry and Diana walked in yonder alleys," replied Nero. "I believe they were here when the Roman legions conquered Gaul. One thing seems as likely as the other, doesn't it, Poppæa?"

"I don't know about that : but I like to think they are intensely old," answered Daphne, leaning on the iron railing, and looking down at the fish, which were already competing for her favours, feeling assured she meant to feed them.

The old woman got up from her stool, and came over to ask if the young lady would like some bread for the carp.

"Yes, please—a lot," cried Daphne, and she began to fumble in her pocket for the little purse with its three or four francs and half-francs.

The stranger tossed a franc to the woman before Daphne's hand could get to the bottom of her pocket, and the bread was forthcoming—a large hunch off a long loaf. Daphne began eagerly to feed the fish. They were capital fun, disputing vehemently for her bounty, huge gray creatures which looked centuries old—savage, artful, vicious exceedingly. She gave them each a name. One she called Francis, another Henry, another Diana, another Catherine. She was as pleased and amused as a child, now throwing her bit of bread as far as her arm could fling it, and laughing merrily at the eager rush of competitors, now luring them close to the rails, and smiling down at the gray snouts yawning for their prey.

"Do you think they would eat me if I were to tumble in among them?" asked Daphne. "Greedy creatures! They seem ravenous enough for anything. There! they have devoured all my bread."

"Shall I buy you some more?"

"Please, no. This kind of thing might go on for ever. They are insatiable. You would be ruined."

"Shall we go under the trees?"

"If you like. But don't you think this sunshine delicious? It is so nice to bask. I think I am rather like a cat in my enjoyment of the sun."

"Your friend seems to have had enough of it,"

said Nero, glancing towards a sheltered bench to which Miss Dibb had discreetly withdrawn herself.

"Martha! I had almost forgotten her existence. The carp are so absorbing."

"Let us stay in the sunshine. We can rejoin your friend presently. She has taken out her needlework, and seems to be enjoying herself."

"Another strip of her everlasting counterpane," said Daphne. "That girl's persevering industry is maddening. It makes one feel so abominably idle. Would you be very shocked to know that I detest needlework?"

"I should as soon expect a butterfly to be fond of needlework as you," answered Nero. "Let me see your hand."

She had taken off her glove to feed the carp, and her hand lay upon the iron rail, dazzlingly white in the sunshine; Nero took it up in his, so gently, so reverently, that she could not resent the action. He took it as a priest or physician might have taken it; altogether with a professional or scientific air.

"Do you know that I am a student of chiromancy?" he asked.

"How should I, when I don't know anything about you? And I don't even know what chiromancy is."

"The science of reading fate and character from the configuration of the hand."

"Why, that is what gipsies pretend to do," cried Daphne. "You surely cannot believe in such nonsense."

"I don't know that my belief goes very far; but I have found the study full of interest, and more than once I have stumbled upon curious truths."

"So do the most ignorant gipsy fortune-tellers," retorted Daphne. "People who are always guessing must sometimes guess right. But you may tell my fortune all the same, please; it will be more amusing than the carp."

"If you approach the subject in such an irreverent spirit, I don't think I will have any-thing to say to you. Remember, I have gone into this question thoroughly, from a scientific point of view."

"I am sure you are wonderfully clever," said

Daphne; and then, in a coaxing voice, with a lovely look from the sparkling gray eyes, she pleaded: "Pray tell my fortune. I shall be wretched if you refuse."

"And I should be wretched if I were to disoblige you. Your left hand, please, and be serious, for it is a very solemn ordeal."

She gave him her left hand. He turned the soft rosy childish palm to the sunlight, and pored over it as intently as if it had been some manuscript treatise of Albertus Magnus, written in cypher, to be understood only by the hierophant in science.

"You are of a fitful temper," he said, "and do not make many friends. Yet you are capable of loving intensely—one or two persons perhaps, not more; indeed, I think only one at a time, for your nature is concentrative rather than diffuse."

He spoke slowly and deliberately—coldly indifferent as an antique oracle—with his eyes upon her hand all the time. He took no note of the changes in her expressive face, which would have told him that he had hit the truth.

"You are apt to be dissatisfied with life."

"Oh, indeed I am," she cried, with a weary sigh; "there are times when I do so hate my life and all things belonging to me—except just one person—that I would change places with any peasant-girl trudging home from market."

"You are romantic, variable. You do not care for beaten paths, and have a hankering for the wild and strange. You love the sea better than the land, the night better than the day."

"You are a wizard," cried Daphne, remembering her wild delight in the dancing waves as she stood on the deck of the Channel steamer, her intense love of the winding river at home—the deep, rapid stream—and of fresh salt breezes, and a free ocean life; remembering too how her soul had thrilled with rapture in the shadowy courtyard last night, when her shuttlecock flew up towards the moon. "You have a wonderful knack of finding out things," she said. "Go on, please."

He had dropped her hand suddenly, and was looking up at her with intense earnestness.

"Please go on," she repeated impatiently.

"I have done. There is no more to be told."

"Nonsense. I know you are keeping back something; I can see it in your face. There is something unpleasant—or something strange—I could see it in the way you looked at me just now. I insist upon knowing everything."

"Insist! I am only a fortune-teller so far as it pleases me. Do you think if a man's hand told me that he was destined to be hanged, I should make him uneasy by saying so?"

"But my case is not so bad as that?"

"No; not quite so bad as that," he answered lightly, trying to smile.

The whole thing seemed more or less a joke; but there are some natures so sensitive that they tremble at the lightest touch; and Daphne felt uncomfortable.

"Do tell me what it was," she urged earnestly.

"My dear child, I have no more to tell you. The hand shows character rather than fate. Your character is as yet but half developed. If you want a warning, I would say to you: Beware of the strength of your own nature. In that lies your greatest danger. Life is easiest to those who can take it lightly—who can bend their backs to any burden, and be grateful for every ray of sunshine."

"Yes," she answered contemptuously; "for the drudges. But please tell me the rest. I know you read something in these queer little lines and wrinkles," scrutinising her pink palm as she spoke, "something strange and startling— for you were startled. You can't deny that."

"I am not going to admit or deny anything," said Nero, with a quiet firmness that conquered her, resolute as she was when her own pleasure or inclination was in question. "The oracle has spoken. Make the most you can of his wisdom."

"You have told me nothing," she said, pouting, but submissive.

"And now let us go out of this bakery, under the trees yonder, where your friend looks so happy with her crochet-work."

"I think we ought to go home," hesitated Daphne, not in the least as if she meant it.

"Home! nonsense. It isn't one o'clock yet; and you don't dine at one, do you?"

"We dine at six," replied Daphne with dignity, "but we sometimes lunch at half-past one."

"Your luncheon isn't a very formidable affair, is it—hardly worth going home for?"

"It will keep," said Daphne. "If there is anything more to be seen, Martha and I may as well stop and see it."

"There are the gardens, beyond measure lovely on such a day as this; and there is the famous vinery; and, I think, if we could find a very retired spot out of the ken of yonder beardless patrol, I might smuggle in the materials for another picnic."

"That would be too delightful," cried Daphne, clapping her hands in childish glee, forgetful of fate and clairvoyance.

They strolled slowly through the blinding heat towards that cool grove where patient Martha sat weaving her web, as inflexible in her stolid industry as if she had been one of the fatal sisters.

"What have you been doing all this time, Daphne?" she asked, lifting up her eyes as they approached.

"Feeding the carp. You have no idea what fun they are."

"I wonder you are not afraid of a sunstroke."

"I am never afraid of anything, and I love the sun. Come, Martha, roll up that everlasting crochet, and come for a ramble. We are going to explore the gardens, and by-and-by Mr. Nero is going to get us some lunch."

Martha looked at the unknown doubtfully, yet not without favour. She was a good, conscientious girl: but she was fond of her meals, and a luncheon in the cool shade of these lovely groves would be very agreeable. She fancied, too, that the stranger would be a good caterer. He was much more carefully dressed to-day, in a gray travelling suit. Everything about him looked fresh and bright, and suggestive of easy circumstances. She began to think that Daphne was right, and that he was no Bohemian artist, living from hand to mouth, but a gentleman of position, and that it would not be so very awkward to meet him in Regent Street, when she should be shopping with mamma and Jane.

They strolled along the leafy aisle on the margin of the blue bright lake, faintly stirred by lightest zephyrs. They admired the marble figures of nymph and dryad, which Martha thought would have looked better if they had been more elaborately clad.   They wasted half an hour in happy idleness, enjoying the air, the cool umbrage of lime and chestnut, the glory of the distant light yonder on green sward or blue placid lake, enjoying Nature as she should be enjoyed, in perfect carelessness of mind and heart —as Horace enjoyed his Sabine wood, singing his idle praise of Lalage as he wandered, empty of care.

They found at last an utterly secluded spot, where no eye of military or civil authority could reach them.

"Now, if you two young ladies will only be patient, and amuse yourselves here for a quarter of an hour or so, I will see what can be done in the smuggling line," said the unknown.

"I could stay here for a week," said Daphne, establishing herself comfortably on the velvet turf, while Martha pulled out her work-bag and resumed her crochet-hook. "Take your time, Mr. Nero. I am going to sleep."

She threw off her muslin hat, and laid her cheek upon the soft, mossy bank, letting her pale golden hair fall like a veil over her neck and shoulders. They were in the heart of a green *bosquet*, far from the palace, far from the beaten track of tourists. Nero stopped at a curve in the path to look back at the recumbent figure, the sunny falling hair, the exquisite tint of cheek and chin and lips, just touched by the sun-ray glinting through a break in the foliage. He stood for a few moments admiring this living picture, and then walked slowly down the avenue.

"A curious idle way of wasting a day," he mused; "but when a man has nothing particular to do with his days he may as well waste them one way as another. How lovely the child is in her imperfection! a faulty beauty—a faulty nature —but full of fascination. I must write a description of her in my next letter to my dear one. How interested she would feel in this childish, undisciplined character."

But somehow when his next letter to the lady of his love came to be written he was in a lazy mood, and did not mention Daphne. The subject, to be interesting, required to be treated in detail, and he did not feel himself equal to the task.

"Isn't he nice?" asked Daphne, when the unknown had departed.

"He is very gentlemanlike," assented Martha, "but still I feel we are doing wrong in encouraging him."

"Encouraging him!" echoed her schoolfellow. "You talk as if he were a stray cur that had followed us."

"You perfectly well know what I mean, Daphne. It cannot be right to get acquainted with a strange gentleman as we have done. I wouldn't have mamma or Jane know of it for the world."

"Then don't tell them," said Daphne, yawning

listlessly, and opening her rosy palm for a nonde-
script green insect to crawl over it.

"But it seems such a want of candour," objected
Martha.

"Then tell them, and defy them. But whatever you do, don't be fussy, you dear good-natured
old Martha; for of all things fussiness is the most
detestable in hot weather. As for Mr. Nero, he
will be off and away across the Jura before to-
morrow night, I daresay, and he will forget us,
and we shall forget him, and the thing will be all
over and done with. I wish he would bring us our
luncheon. I'm hungry."

"I feel rather faint," admitted Martha, who
thought it ungenteel to confess absolute hunger.
"That bread we get for breakfast is all sponginess.
Shall you tell your sister about Mr. Nero?"

"That depends. I may, perhaps, if I should
be hard up for something to say to her."

"Don't you think she would be angry?"

"She never is angry. She is all sweetness and
goodness, and belief in other people. I have spent
very little of my life with her, or I should be

ever so much better than I am. I should have
grown up like her perhaps—or just a little like
her, for I'm afraid the clay is different—if my
father would have let me be brought up at
home."

"And he wouldn't?" asked Martha.

She had heard her friend's history very often,
or as much of it as Daphne cared to tell, but
she was always interested in the subject, and
encouraged her schoolfellow's egotism. Daphne's
people belonged to a world which Miss Dibb could
never hope to enter; though perhaps Daphne's
father, Sir Vernon Lawford, had no larger income
than Mr. Dibb, whose furniture and general surroundings were the best and most gorgeous that
money could buy.

"No. When I was a little thing I was sent
to a lady at Brighton, who kept a select school
for little things; because my father could not bear
a small child about the house. When I grew too
tall for my frocks, and was all stocking and long
hair, I was transferred to a very superior establishment at Cheltenham, because my father could not

be worried by the spectacle of an awkward growing girl. When I grew still taller, and was almost a young woman, I was packed off to Madame Tolmache to be finished; and I am to be finished early next year, I believe, and then I am to go home, and my father will have to endure me."

" How nice for you to go home for good! And your home is very beautiful, is it not?" asked Martha, who had heard it described a hundred times.

" It is a lovely house in Warwickshire, all amongst meadows and winding streams—a long, low, white house, don't you know, with no end of verandahs and balconies. I have been there very little, as you may imagine, but I love the dear old place all the same."

" I don't think I should like to live so far in the country," said Martha: " Clapham is so much nicer."

" *Connais pas*," said Daphne indifferently.

The unknown came sauntering back along the leafy arcade, but not alone; an individual quite as fashionably clad, and of appearance as gentle-manlike, walked a pace or two behind him.

"Well, young ladies, I have succeeded splendidly as a smuggler; but I thought two could bring more than one, so I engaged an ally. Now, Dickson, produce the Cliquot."

The individual addressed as Dickson took a gold-topped pint bottle out of each side-pocket. He then, from some crafty lurking-place, drew forth a crockery encased pie, some knives and forks, and a couple of napkins, while Nero emptied his own pockets, and spread their contents on the turf. He had brought some wonderful cherries—riper and sweeter-looking than French fruit usually is—several small white paper packages which sug-gested confectionery, a tumbler, and half-a-dozen rolls, which he had artfully disposed in his various pockets.

"We must have looked rather bulky," he said; "but I suppose the custodians of the place were too sleepy to take any notice of us. The nippers, Dickson? Yes! Thoughtful man! You can come back in an hour for the bottles and the pie-dish."

Dickson bowed respectfully and retired.

"Is that your valet?" asked Daphne.

"He has the misfortune to fill that thankless office."

Daphne burst out laughing.

"And you travel with your own servant?" she exclaimed. "It is too absurd! Do you know that yesterday I took you for a poor strolling artist, and I felt that it would be an act of charity to give you half-a-guinea for that sketch?"

"You would not have obtained it from me for a thousand half-guineas. No; I do not belong to the hard-up section of humanity. Perhaps many a penniless scamp is a better and happier man than I; but, although poverty is the school for heroes, I have never regretted that it was not my lot to be a pupil in that particular academy. And now, young ladies, fall to, if you please. Here is a Perigord pie, which I am assured is the best that Strasbourg can produce, and here are a few pretty tiny kickshaws in the way of pastry; and here, to wash these trifles down, is a bottle of the Widow Cliquot's champagne."

"I don't know that I ever tasted champagne in my life."

"How odd!" cried Martha. "What, not at juvenile parties?"

"I have never been at any juvenile parties."

"We have it often at home," said Martha, with a swelling consciousness of belonging to wealthy people. "At picnics, and whenever there is company to luncheon. The grown-ups have it every evening at dinner, if they like. Papa takes a particular pride in his champagne."

They grouped themselves upon the grass, hidden from all the outside world by rich summer foliage, much more alone than they had been yesterday in the heart of the forest. Honest Martha Dibb, who had been sorely affronted at the free-and-easiness of yesterday's simple meal, offered no objection to the luxurious feast of to-day. A man who travelled with his valet could not be altogether an objectionable person. The whole thing was unconventional—slightly incorrect, even—but there was no longer any fear that they were making friends

with a vagabond, who might turn up in after life
and ask for small loans.

"He is evidently a gentleman," thought Martha,
quite overcome by the gentility of the valet.   "I
daresay papa and mamma would be glad to know
him."

Her spirits enlivened by the champagne, Miss
Dibb became talkative.

"Do you know Clapham Common?" she asked
the stranger.

"I have heard of such a place.   I believe I
have driven past it occasionally on my way to
Epsom," he answered listlessly, with his eyes on
Daphne, who was seated in a lazy attitude, her
back supported by the trunk of a lime-tree, her
head resting against the brown bark, which made
a sombre background for her yellow hair, her
arms hanging loose at her sides in perfect restfulness, her face and attitude alike expressing a
dreamy softness, as of one for whom the present
hour is enough, and all time and life beyond it
no more than a vague dream.   She had just touched

the brim of the champagne glass with her lips
and that was all. She had pronounced the Perigord
pie the nastiest thing that she had ever tasted;
and she had lunched luxuriously upon pastry and
cherries.

"I live on Clapham Common, when I am at
home," said Martha. "Papa has bought a large
house, with a Corinthian portico, and we have ever
so many hot-houses. Papa takes particular pride
in his grapes and pines. Are you fond of pines?"

"Not particularly," answered Nero, stifling a
yawn. "And where do you live when you are
at home, my pretty Poppæa?" he asked, smiling
at Daphne, who had lifted one languid arm to
convey a ripe red cherry to lips that were as fresh
and rosy as the fruit.

"In Oxford Street," answered Daphne coolly.

Miss Dibb's eyebrows went up in horrified
wonder; she gave a little gasp, as who should
say, "This is too much!" but did not venture a
contradiction.

"In Oxford Street? Why, that is quite a
business thoroughfare. Is your father in trade?"

"Yes. He keeps an Italian warehouse."

Martha became red as a turkey-cock. This was a liberty which she felt she ought to resent at once; but, sooth to say, the matter-of-fact Martha had a wholesome awe of her friend. Daphne was very sweet; Daphne and she were sworn allies; but Daphne had a sharp tongue, and could let fly little shafts of speech, half playful, half satiric, that pierced her friend to the quick.

"I hope there is nothing that I need be ashamed of in my father's trade," she said gravely.

"Of course not," faltered the stranger. "Trade is a most honourable employment of capital and intelligence. I have the greatest respect for the trading classes—but——"

"But you seemed surprised when I told you my father's position."

"Yes; I confess that I was surprised. You don't look like a tradesman's daughter, somehow. If you had told me that your father was a painter, or a poet, or an actor even, I should have thought it the most natural thing in the world. You look as if you were allied to the arts."

"Is that a polite way of saying that I don't look quite respectable?"

"I am not going to tell you what I mean. You would say I was paying you compliments, and I believe you have tabooed all compliments. I may be ruder than Petruchio—didn't you tell me so in the forest yesterday?—but any attempt at playing Sir Charles Grandison will be resented."

"I certainly like you best when you are rude," answered Daphne.

She was not as animated as she had been yesterday during their homeward walk. The heat and the supreme stillness of the spot invited silence and repose. She was, perhaps, a little tired by the exploration of the *château*. She sat under the drooping branches of the lime, whose blossoms sweetened all the air, half in light, half in shadow: while Martha, who had eaten a hearty luncheon, and consumed nearly a pint of Cliquot, plodded on with her crochet-work, and tried to keep the unknown in conversation.

She asked him if he had seen this, and that, and the other—operas, theatres, horticultural fêtes

—labouring hard to make him understand that her people were in the very best society—as if opera-boxes and horticultural fêtes meant society! and succeeded only in boring him outrageously.

He would have been content to sit in dreamy silence watching Daphne eat her cherries. Such an occupation seemed best suited to the sultry summer silence, the perfumed atmosphere.

But Martha thought silence must mean dulness.

"We are dreadfully quiet to-day," she said. "We must do something to get the steam up. Shall we have some riddles? I know lots of good ones that I didn't ask you yesterday."

"Please don't," cried Nero; "I am not equal to it. I think a single conundrum would crush me. Let us sit and dream.

> How sweet it were, hearing the downward stream,
> With half-shut eyes ever to seem
> Falling asleep in a half-dream!
> To dream and dream, like yonder amber light,
> Which will not leave the myrrh-bush on the height."

Martha looked round inquiringly. She did not see either myrrh-bush or height in the landscape.

They were in a level bit of the park, shut in by trees.

" Is that poetry ? " she asked.

" Well, it's the nearest approach to it that the last half-century has produced," replied the unknown, and then he went on quoting :

> " But propt on beds of amaranth and moly,
> How sweet (while warm airs lull us blowing lowly)
> With half-dropt eyelids still,
> Beneath a heaven dark and holy,
> To watch the long bright river drawing slowly
> His waters from the purple hill.

Poppæa, I wish you and I were queen and king of a Lotos Island, and could idle away our lives in perpetual summer."

" We should soon grow tired of it," answered Daphne. " I am like the little boy in the French story-book. I delight in all the seasons. And I daresay you skate, hunt, and do all manner of things that couldn't be done in summer."

" True, my astute empress. But when one is sitting under lime-boughs on such a day as this, eternal summer seems your only idea of happiness."

He gave himself up to idle musing. Yes; he was surprised, disappointed even, at the notion of this bright-haired nymph's parentage. There was no discredit in being a tradesman's daughter. He was very far from feeling a contempt for commerce. There were reasons in his own history why he should have considerable respect for successful trade. But for this girl he had imagined a different pedigree. She had a high-bred air—even in her reckless unconventionality—which accorded ill with his idea of a prosperous tradesman's daughter. There was a poetry in her every look and movement, a wild untutored grace, which was the strangest of all flowers to have blossomed in a parlour behind a London shop. Reared in the smoke and grime of Oxford Street! Brought up amidst ever present considerations of pounds, shillings, and pence! The girl and her surroundings were so incongruous that the mere idea of them worried him.

"And by-and-by she will marry some bloated butcher or pompous coach-builder, and spend all her days among the newly rich," he thought.

"She will grow into the fat wife of a fat alderman, and overdress and overeat herself, and live a life of prosperous vulgarity."

The notion was painful to him, and he was obliged to remind himself that there was very little likelihood of his ever seeing this girl again, so that the natural commonplaceness of her fate could make very little difference to him.

"Better to be vulgarly prosperous and live to be a great-grandmother than to fulfil the prophecy written on her hand," he said to himself. "What does it matter? Let us enjoy to-day, and let the long line of to-morrows rest in the shadow that wraps the unknown future. To-morrow I shall be on my way to Geneva, panting and stifling in a padded railway-carriage, with oily Frenchmen, who will insist upon having the windows up through the heat and dust of the long summer day, and I shall look back with envy to this delicious afternoon."

They sat under the limes for a couple of hours, talking a little now and then in a desultory way; Martha trying her hardest to impress the unknown with the grandeurs and splendours of Lebanon Lodge, Clapham Common; Daphne saying very little, content to sit in the shade and dream. Then, having taken their fill of rest and shadow, they ventured out into the sun, and went to see the famous grapery, and then Martha looked at her watch and protested that they must go home to tea. Miss Toby would be expecting them.

Nero went with them to the gates of the palace, and would fain have gone further, but Daphne begged him to leave them there.

"You would only frighten our poor governess," she said. "She would think it quite a terrible thing for us to have made your acquaintance. Please go back to your hotel at once."

"If you command me to do so, I must obey," said Nero politely.

He shook hands with them for the first time, gravely lifted his hat, and walked across to his hotel. It was on the opposite side of the way, a big white house, with a garden in front of it, and a fountain playing. The two girls stood in the shadow watching him.

"He is really very nice," said Martha. "I think mamma would like to have him at one of her dinner-parties. But he did not tell us anything about himself, did he?"

Daphne did not hear her. There was hardly room in that girlish brain for all the thoughts that were crowding into it.

CHAPTER IV.

"CURTEIS SHE WAS, DISCRETE, AND DEBONAIRE."

The world was nine months older since Daphne picnicked in the park at Fontainebleau, and the scenery of her life was changed to a fair English landscape in one of the fairest of English shires. Here, in fertile Warwickshire, within three miles of Shakespeare's birthplace, within a drive of Warwick and Leamington, and Kenilworth, and Stoneleigh Park, to say nothing of ribbon-weaving, watch-making Coventry, Daphne wandered in happy idleness through the low-lying water meadows, which bounded the sloping lawns and shady gardens of South Hill.

South Hill was a gentle elevation in the midst

of a pastoral valley. A long, low, white house, which had been added to from time to time, crowned the grassy slope, and from its balconied windows commanded one of the prettiest views in England—a landscape purely pastoral and rustic; low meadows through which the Avon wound his silvery way between sedgy banks, with here a willowy islet, and there a flowery creek. On one side the distant roofs and gables and tall spire of Stratford, seen above intervening wood and water; on the other a gentle undulating landscape, bounded by a range of hills purple with distance.

It was not an old house. There was nothing historical about it; though South Hill, with between three and four hundred acres, had belonged to Sir Vernon Lawford's family since the reign of Elizabeth. There had been an ancient mansion; but the ancient mansion, being an unhealthy barrack of small low rooms, and requiring the expenditure of five thousand pounds to make it healthy and habitable, Sir Vernon's father had conceived the idea that he could make a better use of his money if he pulled down the old house and built himself a new one: whereupon the venerable pile was demolished, much to the disgust of archæologists, and an Italian villa rose from its ashes: a house with wide French windows opening into broad verandahs, delicious places in which to waste a summer morning, or the idle after-dinner-hour watching the sunset. All the best rooms at South Hill faced the south-west, and the sunsets there seemed to Madoline Lawford more beautiful than anywhere else in the world. It was a house of the simplest form, built for ease and comfort rather than for architectural display. There were long cool corridors, lofty rooms below and above stairs, a roomy hall, a broad shallow staircase, and at one end of the house a spacious conservatory which had been added by Sir Vernon soon after his marriage. This conservatory was the great feature of South Hill. It was a lofty stone building, with a double flight of marble steps descending from the drawing-room to the billiard-room below. Thus drawing-room and billiard-room both commanded a full view of the conservatory through wide glass doors.

There were melancholy associations for Sir

H 2

Vernon Lawford in this wing which he had added
to South Hill.   He had built it to give pleasure to
his first wife, an heiress, and the most amiable of
women : but before the building was finished the
first Lady Lawford was in her grave, leaving a baby
girl of two months old behind her.   The widower
grieved intensely ; but he proved no exception to
the general rule that the more intense the sorrow
of the bereaved the more speedily does he or she
seek consolation in new ties.   Sir Vernon married
again within two years of his wife's death ; and, this
time, instead of giving satisfaction to the county by
choosing one of the best born and wealthiest ladies
within its length and breadth, he picked up his wife
somewhere on the Continent--a fact which in the
opinion of the county was much in her disfavour—
and when he brought her home and introduced her
to his friends, he was singularly reticent as to her
previous history.

The county people shrugged their shoulders, and
doubted if this marriage would end well.   They had
some years later the morbid satisfaction of being able
to say that they had prophesied aright.   The second

Lady Lawford bore her husband two children, a boy and a girl, and within a year of her daughter's birth mysteriously disappeared. She went to the South of France, it was said, for her lungs; though everybody's latest recollection of her was of a young woman in the heyday of health, strength, and beauty; somewhat self-willed, very extravagant, inordinately fond of pleasure, and governing her husband with the insolence of conscious beauty.

From that southern journey she never came back. Nobody ever heard any explicit account of her death; yet after two or three years it became an accepted fact that she was dead. Sir Vernon travelled a good deal, while his maiden sister kept house for him at South Hill, and superintended the rearing of his children. Madoline, daughter and heiress of the first Lady Lawford, was brought up and educated at home. Loftus, the boy, went to a private tutor at Stratford, and thence to Rugby, where he fell ill and died. Daphne's childhood and early girlhood were spent almost entirely at school. Only a week ago she was still at Asnières, grinding away at the everlasting prosy old books, reciting

Lafontaine's fables, droning out long sing-song speeches from Athalie or Iphigénie, teasing poor patient Miss Toby, domineering over Martha Dibb. And now her education was supposed to be finished, and she was free—free to roam like a wild thing about the lovely grounds at South Hill, in the water-meadows where the daffodils grew in such rank luxuriance; and where, years ago, when she was a little child, and had crowned herself with a chaplet of those yellow flowers, scarcely brighter than her hair, a painter-friend of her father's had called her Asphodel.

How well she remembered that sunny morning in early April—ages ago! Childhood seems so far off at seventeen. How distinctly she remembered the artist whose refined and gentle manners had won her childish heart! She had been so little praised at South Hill that her pulses thrilled with pleasure when her father's friend smiled at her flower-crowned head and cried: "What a lovely picture! Look, Lawford, would not you like me to paint her just as she is at this moment, with her hair flying in the wind, and that background of

rushes and blue water?" But Sir Vernon turned on
his heel with a curt half-muttered answer, and the
two men walked on and left her, smoking their
cigarettes as they went. She remembered how, in
a blind childish fury, scarce knowing why she was
angry, she tore the daffodil crown from her hair and
trampled it under foot.

To the end of his visit the painter called her
Asphodel, and one morning finding her alone in the
garden, he carried her off to the billiard-room and
made a sketch of her head with its loose tangled
hair : a head which appeared next year on the line
at the Royal Academy and was raved about by all
artistic London.

And now it was early April again, and she was
a girl in the fair dawn of womanhood, free to do
what she liked with her life, and there were many
things that she was beginning to understand, things
not altogether pleasant to her womanly pride. She
was beginning to perceive very clearly that her father
did not love her, and was never likely to love her,
that her presence in his home gave him no pleasure,
that he simply endured her as part of the burden

of life, while to her sister he gave love without stint
or measure. True that he was by nature and habit
selfish and self-indulgent, and that the love of such
a man is at best hardly worth having. But Daphne
would have been glad of her father's love, were the
affection of ever so poor a quality. His indifference
chilled her soul. She had been accustomed to command affection ; to be petted and praised and bowed
down to for her pretty looks and pretty ways ; to
take a leading position with her schoolfellows, partly
because she was Sir Vernon Lawford's daughter,
and partly for those subtle charms and graces
which made her superior to the rank and file of
school-girls.

Yet, though Sir Vernon was wanting in affection
for his younger daughter, Daphne was not unloved
at South Hill. Her sister Madoline loved her
dearly, had so loved her ever since those un-
forgotten summer days when the grave girl of
nine and the toddling two-year-old baby wandered
hand-in-hand in shrubberies and gardens, and
seemed to have the whole domain of South Hill to
themselves, Sir Vernon and Lady Lawford being

somewhere on the Continent, and the maiden
aunt being a lady very much in request in the
best society in the neighbourhood, and very
willing to take the utmost enjoyment out of life,
and to delegate her duties to nurses and maids.
The love that had grown up in those days between
the sisters had been in no wise lessened by sever-
ance. They were as devoted to each other now
as they had been in the dawn of life: Madoline
loving Daphne with a proud protecting love;
Daphne looking up to Madoline with intense
respect, and believing in her as the most perfect
of women.

"I'm afraid I shall never be able to leave off
talking," said Daphne upon this particular April
morning, when she had come in from a long ramble
by the Avon, with her apron full of daffodils; "I
seem to have such a world of things to tell
you."

"Don't put any check upon your eloquence,
darling. You won't tire me," said Madoline in her
low gentle voice.

She had a very soft voice, and a slow, calm way

of speaking, which seemed to most people to be the true patrician tone. She spoke like a person who had never been in a hurry, and had never been in a passion.

The sisters were in Madoline's morning-room, sometimes called the old drawing-room, as it had been the chief reception-room at South Hill before Sir Vernon built the west wing. It was a large airy room, painted white, with chintz draperies of the lightest and most delicate tints—apple-blossoms on a creamy ground; the furniture all of light woods; the china celadon or turquoise; but the chief beauty of the room, its hot-house flowers—tulips, gardenias, arums, hyacinths, pansies, grouped with exquisite taste on tables and in jardinières, on brackets and mantelpiece. The love of flowers was almost a passion with Madoline Lawford, and she was rich enough to indulge this inclination to her heart's content. She had built a long line of hot-houses in one of the lower gardens, and kept a small regiment of gardeners and boys. She could afford to do this, and yet to be Lady Bountiful in all the district round about South Hill; so nobody ventured to

blame her for the money she spent upon horticulture.

She was a very handsome woman—handsome in
that perfectly regular style about which there can
be no difference of opinion. Some might call her
beauty cold, but all must own she was beautiful.
Her profile was strongly marked, the forehead
high and broad, the nose somewhat aquiline; the
mouth proud, calm, resolute, yet infinitely sweet
when she smiled; the eyes almost black, with
long dark lashes, sculptured eyelids, and delicately
pencilled brows. She wore her hair as she
might have worn it had she lived in the days of
Pericles and Aspasia—simply drawn back from her
forehead, and twisted in a heavy Greek knot at the
back of her head; no fringed locks or fluffiness
gave their factitious charm to her face. Her beauty
was of that calm statuesque type which has nothing
to do with chic, piquancy, dash, audacity, or any of
those qualities which go such a long way in the
composition of modern loveliness.

All her tastes were artistic; but her love of art
showed itself rather in the details of daily life than

in any actual achievement with brush or pencil. She worked exquisitely in crewels and silks, drew her own designs from natural flowers, and produced embroideries on linen or satin which were worthy to be hung in a picture-gallery. She had a truly feminine love of needlework, and was never idle— in this the very reverse of Daphne, who loved to loll at ease, looking lazily at the sky or the landscape, and making up her mind to be tremendously busy by-and-by. Daphne was always beginning work, and never finishing anything; while every task undertaken by Madoline was carried on to completion. The very essence of her own character was completeness—fulfilling every duty to the uttermost, satisfying in fullest measure every demand which home or society could make upon her.

"I'm sure you'll be tired of me, Lina," protested Daphne, kneeling on the fender-stool, while Madoline sat at work in her accustomed place, with a Japanese bamboo table at her side for the accommodation of her crewels. "You can't imagine what a capacity I have for talking."

"Then I must be very dull," murmured Madoline, smiling at her. "You have been home a week."

"Well, certainly, you have had some experience of me; but you might think my loquacity a temporary affliction, and that when I had said my say after nearly two years of separation—oh, Lina, how horrid it was spending all my holidays at Asnières!—I should subside into comparative silence. But I shall always have worlds to tell you. It is my nature to say everything that comes into my mind. That's why I got on so well with Dibb."

"Was Dibb a dog, dear?"

"A dog!" cried Daphne, with a sparkling smile. "No, Dibb was my schoolfellow—a dear good thing—stupid, clumsy, innately vulgar, but devoted to me. 'A poor thing, but mine own,' as Touchstone says. We were tremendous chums."

"I am sorry you should make a friend of any innately vulgar girl, Daphne dear," said Madoline gravely; "and don't you think it rather vulgar to talk of your friend as Dibb?"

"We all did it," answered Daphne with a shrug; "I was always called Lawford. It saves trouble, and sounds friendly. You talk about Disraeli and Gladstone; why not Dibb and Lawford?"

"I think there's a difference, Daphne. If you were very friendly with this Miss Dibb, why not speak of her by her christian name?"

"So be it, my dearest. In future she shall be Martha, to please you. She really is a good inoffensive soul. Her father keeps a big shop in Oxford Street; but the family live in a palace on Clapham Common, with gardens, and vineries, and pineries, and goodness knows what. When I call her vulgar it is because she and all her people are so proud of their money, and measure everything by the standard of money. Martha was very inquisitive about my means. She wanted to know whether I was rich or poor, and I really couldn't inform her. Which am I, Lina?"

Daphne looked up at her sister as if it were a question about which she was slightly curious, but not a matter of supreme moment. A faint

flush mounted to Madoline's calm **brow. The**
soft dark eyes looked tenderly at Daphne's eager
face.

"Dearest, why trouble yourself about the
money question ? **Have** you **ever felt** the in-
convenience of poverty ? "

"Never. You sent me everything **I could**
possibly wish for; and I always had more pocket-
money than **any girl** in the school, not excepting
Martha ; though she took care to inform me that
her father could have allowed her ten times as
much if he had chosen. No, dear ; I don't know
what poverty means ; but I should like to understand my own position very precisely, now that I
am a woman, don't you know ? **I** am quite
aware that you are an heiress ; everybody at
South Hill has taken pains to impress that fact
upon my mind. Please, dear, what am **I ? "**

" Darling, papa is not a rich man, but he——"
Madoline paled a little as she spoke, knowing
that South Hill had been settled on her mother,
and her mother's children after her, and that, in
all probability, Sir Vernon **had** hardly **any other**

property in the world. "He will provide for you, no doubt. And if he were unable to leave you much by-and-by, I have plenty for both."

"I understand," said Daphne, growing pale in her turn; "I am a pauper."

"Daphne!"

"My mother had not a sixpence, I suppose; and that is why nobody ever speaks of her; and that is why there is not a portrait of her in this house, where she lived, and was admired, and loved. I was wrong to call Dibb vulgar for measuring all things by a money standard. It is other people's measure, as well as hers."

"Daphne, how can you say such things?"

"Didn't I tell you that I say everything that comes into my head? Oh, Madoline, don't for pity's sake think that I envy you your wealth— you who have been so good to me, you who are all I have to love in this world! It is not the money I care for. I think I would just as soon be poor as rich, if I could be free to roam the world, like a man. But to live in a great house, waited on by an army of servants, and to know that I am nobody, of no account, a mere waif, the penniless daughter of a penniless mother— that wounds me to the quick."

"My dearest, my pet, what a false, foolish notion! Do you think anybody in this house values you less because I have a fortune tied to me by all manner of parchment deeds, and you have no particular settlement, and have only expectations from a not over-rich father? Do you think you are not admired for your grace and pretty looks, and that by-and-by there will not come the best substitute which modern life can give for the prince of our dear old fairy tales —a good husband, who will be wealthy enough to give my darling all she can desire in this world?"

"I'm sure I shall hate him, whoever he may be," said Daphne, with a short, impatient sigh.

Madoline looked at her earnestly, with the tender motherly look which came naturally to the beautiful face when the elder sister looked at the younger. She had put aside her crewel-work at the beginning of this conversation, and had given all her attention to Daphne.

"Why do you say that, dearest?" she asked gravely.

"Oh, I don't know, really. But I'm sure I shall never marry."

"Isn't it rather early to make up your mind on that point?"

"Why should it be? Hasn't one a mind and a heart at seventeen as well as at seven-and-twenty? I should like well enough to have a very rich husband by-and-by, so that, instead of being Daphne, the pauper, I might be Mrs. Somebody, with ever-so-much a year settled upon me for ever and ever. But I don't believe I shall ever see anybody I shall be able to care for."

"I hope, darling, you haven't taken it into your foolish head that you care for someone already. School-girls are so silly."

"And generally fall in love with the dancing-master," said Daphne, with a laugh. "I think I tried rather hard to do that, but I couldn't succeed. The poor man wore a wig; a dreadfully natural, dreadfully curly wig; like the pictures of Lord Byron. No, Lina; I pledge you my word that no dancing-master's image occupies my breast."

"I am glad to hear it," answered Madoline. "1 hope there is no one else."

Daphne blushed rosy red. She took a gardenia from the low glass vase on her sister's work-table, where the white waxen flowers were clustered in the centre of a circle of purple pansies, and began to pick the petals off slowly, one by one.

"He loves me—loves me not," she whispered softly, smiling all the while at her own foolishness, till the smile faded slowly at sight of the barren stem.

"Loves me not," she sighed. "You see, Fate is against me, Lina. I am doomed to die unmarried."

"Daphne, do you mean that there is some-one?" faltered Madoline, more in earnest than it might seem needful to be with a creature so utterly childlike.

"There was a man once in a wood," said Daphne, with crimson cheeks and downcast eye-lids, yet with an arch smile curving her lips all the while. "There was a man whom Dibb—I beg your pardon, Martha—and I once met in a wood in our holidays—papa would have me spend my holidays at school, you see—and I have thought since, sometimes—mere idle fancy, no doubt—that he is the only man I should ever care to marry; and that is impossible, for he is engaged to someone else. So you see I am fated to die a spinster."

"Daphne, what do you mean? A man whom you met in a wood, and he was engaged—and——! You don't mean that you and your friend Miss Dibb made the acquaintance of a strange man whom you met when you were out walking," exclaimed Madoline, aghast at the idea. "Surely you were too well looked after for that! You never went out walking alone, did you? I thought Frenchwomen were so extremely particular."

"Of course they are," replied Daphne, laughing. "I was only drawing on my imagination, dearest, just to see that solemn face of yours. It was worth the trouble. No, Lina dear, there is no one. My heart is as free as my shuttlecock,

when I send it flying over the roof scaring the
swallows. And now, let us talk about your dear
self. I want you to tell me all about Mr. Goring;
about Gerald. I suppose I may call him by his
christian name, as he is to be my brother-in-law
by-and-by."

" Your brother, dear."

" Thank you, Lina. That sounds ever so much
nicer. I am so short of relations. Then I shall
always call him Gerald. What a pretty name ! "

" He was called after his mother, Lady
Geraldine."

" I see. She represented the patrician half
of his family, and his father the plebeian half, I
believe ? The father was a Dibb, was he not—a
money-grubber."

" His father was a very worthy man, who
rose from the ranks, and made his fortune as a
contractor."

" And Lady Geraldine married him for the
sake of his worthiness; and you and Gerald are
going to spend his money."

" Mr. Goring and his wife were a very united

couple, I believe, Daphne. There is no reason why you should laugh at them."

"Except my natural malice, which makes me inclined to ridicule good people. You should have said that, Madoline; for you look as if you meant it. Was the contractor's name always Goring?"

"No; he was originally a Mr. Giles, but he changed his name soon after his marriage, and took the name of his wife's maternal grandfather, a Warwickshire squire."

"What a clever way of hooking himself on to the landed gentry!" said Daphne. "And now, please tell me all about Gerald. Is he very nice?"

"You may suppose that I think him so," answered Madoline, going on with the fashioning of a water-lily on a ground of soft gray cloth. "I can hardly trust myself to praise him, for fear I should say too much."

"How is it that I have seen no photograph of him? I expected to see half a dozen portraits of him in this room alone; but I suppose you have an album crammed with his photos some-where under lock and key."

"He has not **been** photographed **since** he was a school-boy. **He detests** photography; **and** though he has **often** promised me that he would sacrifice **his** own feelings so far as to be photographed, he has never kept **his word.**"

"That is very bad of him," said Daphne. "I am bursting with curiosity about **his looks.** But —perhaps," she faltered, with **a deprecating air,** "the poor **thing is rather plain, and that is why** he does not care **to** be photographed."

"**No,**" replied Madoline, **with her gentle smile;** "I do not think his worst enemy could **call him** plain—not that I should love **him less if he were** the plainest of mankind."

"**Yes, you** would," exclaimed Daphne, with conviction. "It **is all very** well **to** talk about loving a man **for** his mind, or **his heart, and all** that kind of thing. You wouldn't love **a man with** a potato-nose **or a** pimply complexion, if he **were** morally the most perfect creature in the universe. I am **very** glad my future brother is handsome."

"That is a matter of opinion—I don't know your idea of a handsome man."

"Let me see," said Daphne, clasping her hands above her head, in a charmingly listless attitude, and giving herself up to thought. "My idea of good looks in a man? The subject requires deliberation. What do you say to a pale complexion, inclining to sallowness; dreamy eyes, under dark straight brows; forehead low, yet broad enough to give room for plenty of brains; mouth grave, and even mournful in expression, except when he smiles—the whole face must light up like a god's when he smiles; hair darkest brown, short, straight, silky?"

"One would think you had seen Mr. Goring, and were describing him," said Madoline.

"What, Lina, is he like that?"

"It is so difficult to realise a description, but really yours might do for Gerald. Yet, I daresay, the image in your mind is totally different from that in mine."

"No doubt," answered Daphne, and then, with a half-breathed sigh, she quoted her favourite Tennyson. "No two dreams are like."

"You will be able to judge for yourself before

long," said Madoline; "Gerald is coming home in the autumn."

"The autumn!" cried Daphne. "That is an age to wait. And then, I suppose, you are to be married immediately?"

"Not till next spring. That is my father's wish. You see, I don't come of age till I'm twenty-five, and there are settlements and technical difficulties. Papa thought it best for us to wait, and I did not wish to oppose him."

"I believe it is all my father's selfishness. He can't bear to lose you."

"Can I be angry with him for that?" asked Madoline, smiling tenderly at the thought of her father's love. "I am proud to think that I am necessary to his happiness."

"But there is your happiness—and Mr. Goring's —to be considered. It has been such a long engagement, and you have been kept so much apart. It must have been a dreary time for you. If ever I am engaged I hope my young man will always be dancing attendance upon me."

"My father thought it best that we should not

be too much together, for fear we should get tired
of each other," said Madoline, with an incredulous
smile; "and as Gerald is very fond of travelling,
and wanted change after the shock of his
mother's death, papa proposed that he should
spend the greater part of his life abroad until my
twenty-fifth birthday. The separation would be
a test for us both, my father thought."

"A most cruel, unjustifiable test," cried Daphne
indignantly. "Your twenty-fifth birthday, for-
sooth! Why, you will be an old woman before
you are married. In all the novels I ever read, the
heroine married before she was twenty, and even
then she seemed sometimes quite an old thing.
Eighteen is the proper age for orange-blossoms
and a Brussels veil."

"That is all a matter of opinion, pet. I don't
think young lady novelists of seventeen and
eighteen have always the wisest views of life.
You must not say a word against your father,
Daphne. He always acts for the best."

"I never heard of a domestic tyrant yet of

whom that could not be said," retorted Daphne. " However, darling, if you are satisfied, I am content; and I shall look forward impatiently to the autumn, and to the pleasure of making my new brother's acquaintance. I hope he will like me."

" No fear of that, Daphne."

" I am not at all sure of winning his regard. Look at my father ! I would give a great deal to be loved by him, yet he detests me."

" Daphne ! How can you say such a thing ? "

" It is the truth. Why should I not say it ? Do you suppose I don't know the signs of aversion as well as the signs of love? I know that you love me. You have no need to tell me so. I do not even want the evidence of your kind acts. I am assured of your love. I can see it in your face; I can hear it in every tone of your voice. And I know just as well that my father dislikes me. He kept me at a distance as long as ever he could, and now that duty—or his regard for other people's opinion—obliges him to have me at home, he avoids me as if I were a roaring lion, or something equally unpleasant."

"Only be patient, dear. You will win his heart in time," said Madoline soothingly. She had put aside the water-lily, and had drawn her sister's fair head upon her shoulder with caressing fondness. "He cannot fail to love my sweet Daphne when he knows her better," she said.

"I don't know that. I fancy he was prejudiced against me when I was a little thing and could scarcely have offended him; unless it were by cutting my teeth disgustingly, or having nettle-rash, or something of that kind. Lina, do you think he hated my mother?"

Madoline started, and flushed crimson.

"Daphne! what a question! Why, my father's second marriage was a love-match, like his first."

"Yes, I suppose he was in love with her, or he would hardly have married a nobody," said Daphne, in a musing tone; "but he might have got to hate her afterwards."

At this moment the door was opened, and a

voice, full, round, manly in tone, said: " Madoline, I want you."

Lina rose hastily, letting her work fall out of her lap, kissed Daphne, and hurried from the room at her father's summons.

CHAPTER V.

MANY a time since her home-coming had Daphne
been on the point of telling her sister all about that
more or less anonymous traveller, whom she called
the man in the wood; but her picnicking adventures,
looked at retrospectively from the strictly-correct
atmosphere of home, seemed much more terrible
than they had appeared to her at Asnières; where
a vague hankering after forbidden pleasures was an
element in the girlish mind, and where there was a
current idea that the most appalling impropriety
was allowable, provided the whole business were
meant as a joke. But Daphne, seated at Madoline's
feet, began to feel doubtful if there were any excuse

for such joking; and, after that one skirmishing
approach to the subject, she said no more about the
gentleman who had called himself Nero. It was
hateful to her to have a secret, were it the veriest
trifle, from her sister; but the idea of Madoline's
disapproval was still more repugnant to her; and
she was very certain that Madoline would disapprove
of the whole transaction in which Mr. Nero had
been concerned.

"I could never tell her how thoroughly at home
I felt with him," mused Daphne; "how easy and
natural our acquaintance seemed—just as if we had
been destined from the very beginning of time to
meet at that hour and at that spot. And to part so
soon!" added Daphne with a sigh. "It seemed
hardly worth while to meet."

Yes; it was a mystery upon which Daphne
brooded very often in the fair spring weather, as
she wandered by her beloved river. Strange that
two lives should meet and touch for a moment, like
circles on yonder placid water—meet, and touch,
and part, and never meet again!

"The rings on the river break when they

touch," thought Daphne. "They are fatal to each other. Our meeting had no significance : two summer days and it was all over and ended. I wonder whether Nero ever thought of Poppæa after he left Fontainebleau ? Poppæa ! What a silly name; and what a simpleton he must have thought me for assuming it."

Of all things at South Hill, where there was so much that was beautiful, Daphne loved the river. It had been her delight when she was a tiny child, hardly able to syllable the words that were meant to express admiration. She had wanted to walk into the water—had struggled in her nurse's arms to get at it, and make herself a part of the thing that seemed so beautiful. Then when she was just a little older and a little wiser, it had been her delight to sit on the very edge of the stream, to sit hidden in the rushes, spelling out a fairy tale. In those early days she would have been happy if the world had begun and ended in those low-lying meadows where daffodils, and orchises, and blue-bells grew in such rich abundance that she could gather and waste them all day long, yet make no perceptible difference in their number; where the lazy cattle stood half the day breast-high in the weedy water, dreaming with wide-open eyes; where the shadow of a bird flitting across the stream was the only thing that gave token of life's restlessness. Later there came a happy midsummer holiday when her father was away at Ems, nursing his last fancied disorder, and she and Madoline were alone together at South Hill under the protection of the maiden aunt, who never interfered with anybody's pleasure so long as she could enjoy her own way of life; and in a willow-shaded creek Daphne found a disused forgotten punt which had lain stagnant in the mud for the last seven years, and with the aid of a youth who worked in the gardens she had so patched and caulked and painted this derelict as to make it tolerably water-tight, and in this frail and clumsy craft she had punted herself up and down a shallow tributary of the deep swift Avon, as far afield as she could go without making Madoline absolutely miserable.

And now being "finished," and a young woman, Daphne asked herself where she was to get a boat.

She had plenty of pocket-money. There was an old boat-house under one of the willows where she could keep her skiff. She had learnt to swim at Asnières, so there could be no danger. So she took counsel with the garden youth, who had grown into a man by this time, and asked him whether he could buy her a boat, and where.

"That's accordin' to the kind o' boat as you might fancy, miss," answered her friend. "There's a many kind o' boats, you see."

"Oh, I hardly know; but I should like something light and pretty, a long, narrow boat, don't you know?" and Daphne went on to describe an outrigger.

"Lord, miss, it would be fearful dangerous. You'd be getting he among the weeds, and upsettin' un. You'd better have a dingey. That's safe and comfortable like."

"A dingey's a thing like a washing-tub, isn't it?"

"Rayther that shape, miss."

"I wouldn't sit in such a thing for the world. No, Bink, if I can't have a long, narrow boat with a sharp nose, I'll have a punt. I think I should really like a punt. I was so fond of that one. feel quite sorry that the rats ate it. Yes; you must buy me a punt. There'll be plenty of room in it for my drawing-board, and my books, and my crewel-work; for I mean to live on the river when the summer comes. How soon can you buy me my punt?"

"I think as how you'd better have a dingey, miss," said Bink. "It was all very well pushing about a punt in the creeks when you was a child, but a punt don't do in deep water. You can have a nice-shaped dingey, not too much of a tub, you know, and a pair o' sculls, and I'll teach you to row. I can order it any arternoon that I can get an 'oliday, miss. There's a good boat-builder at Stratford. I'll order he to build it."

"How lovely," cried Daphne, clapping her hands. "A boat built on purpose for me! It must have no end of cushions, for 'my sister will come with me very often, of course. And it must be painted in the early English style. I'll have a dark red dado."

K 2

"A what, miss?"

"A dado, Bink. The lower half of the inside must be painted dark red, and the upper half a lovely cream colour; and the outside must be a dark greenish-brown. You understand, don't you?"

"Not over well, miss. You'd better write it down for the boat-builder."

"I'll do better than that, Bink—I'll make a sketch of the boat, and paint it the colours I want. And it—she—must have a name, I suppose."

"Boats has names mostly, miss."

"My boat shall not be nameless. I'll call her——" A pause, then a sudden dimpling smile and a bright blush, loveliness thrown away on Bink, who stood at ease leaning on his hoe and staring at the river. "I'll call her—Nero."

"An 'ero, miss. What 'ero? The old Dook o' Wellington? He were an 'ero, warn't he? Or Nelson? That's more of a name for a boat."

"Nero, Bink, Nero. I'll write it down for the boat-builder."

"You'd better, please, miss. I never was good at remembering names."

When Daphne had given Bink the sketch, with full authority to commission her boat, she had an after-thought about her father. The boat-house was his property; even the river in some measure belonged to him; he had at least riparian rights. So after dinner that evening, when Madoline and she were sitting opposite each other in silence at the pretty table, bright with velvety gloxinias and maiden-hair ferns, while Sir Vernon leant back in his chair, sipping his claret, and grumbling vaguely about things in general, the indolence of his servants, the unfitness of his horses, the impending ruin of the land in which he lived, and the crass ignorance of the pig-headed body of men who were pretending to govern it, Daphne, in a pause of the paternal monologue, lifted up her voice.

"Papa, may I have a dingey, please? I can buy it with my own money."

"A dingey!" exclaimed Sir Vernon. "What in Heaven's name is a dingey?"

He had an idea that it must be some article of female attire or of fancy-work, since his frivolous young daughter desired to possess it.

"A dingey—is—a kind of boat, papa."

"Oh, a dingey!" exclaimed Sir Vernon, as if she had said something else in the first instance. "What can you want with a dingey?"

"I am so dearly fond of the river, papa; and a dingey is such a safe boat, Bink says."

"Who is Bink?"

"One of the under gardeners."

"A curious authority to quote. So you want a dingey, and to row yourself about the river like a boy."

"There is no one to notice me, papa."

"The place is secluded enough, so long as you don't go beyond our own meadows. I desired Madame Tolmache to have you taught swimming. Can you swim?"

"Yes, papa. I believe I am a rather good swimmer."

"Well, you can have your boat—it is a horribly masculine taste—always provided you do not go beyond our own fields. I cannot have you boating over half the county."

"I shall be quite happy to keep to our own fields, papa," Daphne answered meekly.

She enlisted the devoted Bink in her service next morning; he patched up the old boat-house, and whitewashed the inside walls; much to the displeasure of Mr. MacCloskie, the head gardener, a gentleman in broadcloth and a top hat, who seemed to do little more than walk about the grounds, smoke his pipe in the hot-houses, plan expensive improvements, and order costly novelties from the most famous nurseries at home and abroad. Bink ought to have been wheeling manure from the stable during that very afternoon which he had devoted to the repair of the boat-house; and Mr. MacCloskie declared that the future well-being of his melon-bed was imperilled by the young man's misconduct.

"I shall complain to Sir Vernon," said Mac-Closkie.

"I beg your pardon, Mr. MacCloskie, but Miss Daphne told me to do it."

"Miss Daphne, indeed! I can't have my

gardeners interfered with by Miss Daphne," exclaimed MacCloskie; as much as to say that his
master's second daughter was a person of very
small account.

He gave Daphne a lecture that evening, in
very broad Scotch, when he met her in the rose-
garden.

"You'll be meddling with my roses next, miss,
I suppose," he said severely. "You young ladies
from boarding-school have no respect for anything."

"Your roses!" cried Daphne, with a con-
temptuous glance at the closely-pruned twigs of
the standards, which at this early period looked
as if they would never flower again. "When I see
any I shall know how to appreciate them. Roses,
indeed! I wonder you like to mention them.
Everything flowers a month earlier in France than
you can make it do here. I had a finer Gloire de
Dijon nodding in at my window at Asnières this
time last year than you ever saw in your life;" and
she marched off, leaving MacCloskie with a dim
idea that in any skirmish with this young lady he
was likely to be worsted.

How ardently she had longed for home a few
weeks ago, when she was counting the days that
must pass before the appointed date of her return,
under the wing of Madame Tolmache, who crossed
the Channel reluctantly once or twice a year to
escort pupils, and was prostrate in the cabin
throughout the brief sea-passage, leaving the
pupils to take care of themselves, and so horribly
ill on landing that the pupils had to take care
of her. So long as South Hill was in the future
Daphne had believed that perfect happiness awaited
her there — gladness without a flaw—but now that
she was at home, established, a recognised member
of the family for all her life to come, she began
to discover that even at South Hill life was not
perfect happiness. She was devotedly fond of
Madoline, and Madoline was full of affection—
careful, anxious, almost maternal love—for her.
There was no flaw in her gladness here. But
every hour she spent in her father's company
made her more certain of the one painful fact
that he did not care for her. There was even in
her mind the terrible suspicion that he actually

disliked her; that he would have been glad to have her out of his way—married, dead and buried —anything so that she might be removed from his path.

She was very young, and her spirits had all the buoyancy of youth that has never been acquainted with sordid cares. So there was plenty of gladness in her life. It was only now and then that the thought of her father's indifference, or possible dislike, drifted like a passing cloud across her mind, and took the charm out of everything.

" What a lovely place it is ! " she said to Madoline, one evening after dinner, when they were strolling about the lawn, where three of the finest deodaras in the county rose like green towers against the warm western sky; " I am fonder of it every day, yet I can't help feeling that I'm an interloper."

" Daphne ! You — the daughter of the house ! "

" A daughter; not the daughter," answered Daphne. " Sometimes I fancy that I am a daughter too many. You should have heard how

MacCloskie talked to me yesterday because I had taken Bink from his work for an hour or two. If I had been a poor little underpaid nursery governess he couldn't have scolded me more severely. And I think servants have a knack of finding out their masters' feelings. If I had been a favourite with my father, MacCloskie would never have talked like that. A favourite! What nonsense! It is so obvious that I bore him awfully."

"Daphne, if you are going to nurse this kind of fancy you will never be happy," Madoline said earnestly, winding her arm round her sister, as they sauntered slowly down the sloping lawn, side by side. "You must make every allowance for papa; he is not a demonstrative man. His manner may seem cold, perhaps——"

"Cold!" cried Daphne; "it is ice. I feel I have entered the frigid zone directly I go into his presence. But he is not cold to you; he has love enough, and to spare, for you."

"We have been so much together. I have learned to be useful to him."

"Yes; you have spent your life with him, while I have been an outcast and an alien."

"Daphne, you have no right to speak like that. My father is a man of peculiar temper. It pleased him to have only one daughter at home till both were grown up. You were more lively than I—younger by seven years—and he fancied you would be noisy. He is a nervous man, wanting an atmosphere of complete repose. And now you are grown up, and have come home for good; and I really cannot see any reason why you should complain."

"No; there is nothing to complain about," cried Daphne bitterly, "only that I have been cheated out of a father's love. Not by you, Lina dearest; no, not by you," she exclaimed, when her sister would have spoken. "I am not base enough to be jealous of you; you, who have been my good angel always. No, dear; but he has cheated me. My father has cheated me in not giving me a chance of getting at his heart when I was a child. What is the good of my trying now? I come home to him as a stranger. How can he be expected to care for me?"

"If he does not love you now, my pet—and mind, I don't admit that it is so—he will soon learn to be fond of you. He can't help admiring my sweet young sister," said Madoline, with tearful eyes.

"I will never plague you about him any more, dear," protested Daphne, with a penitent air. "I will try to be satisfied with your affection. You do love me, don't you?"

"With all my strength."

"And to do my duty in that state of life, etc., etc., etc."

"Talking of duty, Daphne, I have been wanting to make a suggestion for the last week or two," said Madoline gently. "Don't you think it would be better for you if you were to employ yourself a little more?"

"Employ myself!" cried Daphne. "Why, I have been tremendously busy for the last three days—about the dingey."

"Dearest, you are laughing at me. I mean that at seventeen——"

"And a half," interjected Daphne, with dignity.

"At seventeen your education can hardly be completed."

"I know ridiculously little, though I have been outrageously crammed. I'm afraid all the sciences and languages and literature have got mixed up in my brain, somehow," said Daphne; "but I am awfully fond of poetry, I know a good deal of Tennyson by heart. I could repeat every line of 'The Lotos Eaters,' if you asked me," said Daphne, blushing unaccountably.

"I think you ought to read, dear," pursued Madoline gravely.

"Why, so I do. Didn't I read three volumes of 'Sair for Somebody,' in a single day, in order that the book might go back to Mudie's?"

"That rubbishing story! Daphne dear, you know I am talking of serious reading."

"Then you had better find somebody else to talk to," said Daphne. "I never could pin my mind to a dull book; my thoughts go dancing off like butterflies, skimming away like swallows. I could no more plod through a history, or a volume

of 'Voyages in Timbuctoo,' or 'Sir Somebody's
Memoirs at the Court of Queen Joan of Naples,'
or 'A Waiting-woman's Recollections of Peter
the Great,' than I could fly. There are a few
characters in history I like to read about — in
short instalments. Napoleon the Great, for instance.
There is a hero for you — bloodthirsty, but nice.
Mary Stuart, Julius Cæsar, Sir Walter Raleigh,
Columbus, Shakespeare. These shine out like
stars. But the dull dead level of history — the
going out of the Whigs and the coming in of the
Tories, the everlasting battles in the Netherlands
or the Punjaub! I envy you your faculty of
taking interest in such dry-as-dust stuff, but I
cannot imitate you.'

"I like to be able to talk to papa—and to
Gerald, by-and-by," said Madoline shyly.

"Does papa talk of the Punjaub?"

"Not often, dear; but in order to understand
the events of one's own day, it is necessary to
know the history of the past. Papa likes to discuss
public affairs, and I generally read *The Times* to
him every morning, as you know."

"Yes," answered Daphne; "I know you are his slave."

"Daphne, it is my delight to be useful to him."

"Yes; that is the sort of woman you are, always sacrificing your own happiness for other people. But I love you for it, dearest," exclaimed Daphne, with one of her sudden gushes of affection. "Only don't ask me to improve myself, darling, now that I am tasting perfect liberty for the first time in my life. Think how I have been ground and polished and governessed and preached at, and back-boarded," drawing up her slim figure straight as an arrow, "and dumb-belled, and fifth-positioned, for so many weary years of my life, and let me have my fling of idleness at home. I began to wonder if I really had a home, my father kept me away from it so long. Let me be idle and happy, Lina, for a little while; I shall mend by-and-by."

"My pet, do you suppose I don't wish you to be happy. But I don't want your education to come to a full stop, because you have left school."

"Let me learn to be like you, if I can. There could be no higher education than that."

" Flatterer ! "

"No, Lina, no one can flatter perfection."

Madoline stopped her with a kiss, blushing at her praise. And then they turned and walked slowly back to the house, across the dewy lawn, where the shadows of the deodaras had deepened and lengthened with the rising of the moon. Daphne paused on the terrace to look back at the low-lying river gleaming between its willowy banks —so beautiful and ghostly a thing in the moon-light that it almost seemed as if it belonged to another world.

" How lovely it is out of doors ! " sighed Daphne. " Doesn't it seem foolishness to shut oneself up in a house ? Stay a little longer, Lina."

" Papa would not like to be deserted, dear. And Aunt Rhoda talked about coming in this evening."

" Then I am in for a lecture," said Daphne. " Aunt Rhoda told me to go and see her, and I haven't been."

There was a brilliant light in the billiard-room, and the two girls went in through the conservatory and down the marble steps to the room where they were most likely to find their father at this time of the evening. Sir Vernon Lawford was not an enthusiastic billiard-player; indeed, he was not enthusiastic about anything, except his own merits, of which he had a very exalted opinion. He played a game of billiards every evening, because it kept him awake and kept him in gentle movement, which state of being he considered good for his health. He played gravely, as if he were doing his duty to society, and played well; and, though he liked to have his elder daughter in the room while he played, and could bring himself to tolerate the presence of other people, he resented anything distracting in the way of conversation.

Seen in the bright white light of the carcel lamps, Sir Vernon Lawford, at fifty-three years of age, was still a handsome man—a tall, well set-up man, with a hard, clearly chiselled face, eyes of lightish gray, cold and severe in expression, gray hair and whiskers, hands of feminine delicacy in shape and colour, and something rigid and soldier-like in his bearing, as of a man who had been severely drilled himself, and would be a martinet in his rule over others.

He was bending over the table with frowning brow, meditating a difficult stroke, as the two girls came softly in through the wide doorway—two tall slim figures in white gowns, with a background of flowers and palms showing dimly behind them, and beyond the foliage and flowers, the glimmer of a marble balustrade.

A fashionably-dressed lady of uncertain age, the solitary spectator of the game, sat fanning herself in silence by the wide marble fire-place.

Sir Vernon's antagonist came quietly forward to greet Madoline and her sister.

"I am so glad you have come in," he said confidentially. "I am getting ignominiously licked. I had a good mind to throw up the sponge and bolt out into the garden after you just now; only I thought if I didn't take my licking decently, Sir Vernon would never play with me again. Isn't it too delicious out there among the deodaras?"

"Heavenly," exclaimed Daphne; "and the river looks like the *chemin du Paradis*. I wonder you can stay in this glaring room."

Sir Vernon had made up his mind by this time, and with a slow and gentle stroke, made a cannon and sent his adversary's ball into a pocket.

"Just like my luck," said the adversary, while Sir Vernon again deliberated.

He was a man of about seven-and-twenty, tall, broad-shouldered, good-looking, with something of a gladiatorial air in his billiard-room undress. He was fair, with a healthy Saxon colour, and Saxon blue eyes; features not chiselled, but somewhat heavily moulded, yet straight and regular withal; hair, a lightish brown, cropped closely to a well-shaped head; forehead, fairly furnished with intellectual organs, but not the brow of poet or philosopher, wit or savant: a good average English forehead, a good average English face, beaming with good-nature, as he stands by Madoline's side, chalking his cue as industriously as if chalk could win the game.

This   was   Edgar   Turchill,   of   Hawksyard

Grange, Sir Vernon's Lawford's most influential
and pleasantest neighbour, a country squire of old
family and fair fortune, owner of one of the most
interesting places in the county, a real Warwickshire manor-house, and the only son of his widowed
mother.

The lady by the fire-place now began to think
she had been neglected long enough, and beckoned
Daphne with her fan. She beckoned the girl with
an authoritative air which distinctly indicated
relationship.

"Come here and sit by me, child," she whispered,
tapping the fender-stool with the point of her
embroidered shoe, whereupon Daphne meekly
crouched at the lady's feet, prepared for the worst.
" Why have you never been to the Rectory ? "

Daphne twisted her fingers in and out of her
slender watch-chain with an embarrassed air.

" Indeed, I hardly know why, Aunt Rhoda,"
she faltered; "perhaps it was because I was
enjoying myself so much. Everything at home
was so new to me, you see—the gardens, the river,
the meadows."

"You were enjoying yourself so much that you had no inclination to see your aunt and uncle?"

"Uncle?" echoed Daphne. "Oh, you mean the Rector?"

"Of course. Is he not your uncle?"

"Is he, aunt? I know he's your husband; but as you only married him a year ago, and he hadn't begun to be my uncle when I was last at home, it never occurred to me——"

"That by my marriage with him he had become your uncle. That looks like ignorance, Daphne, or want of proper feeling," said the Rector's wife with an offended air.

"It was ignorance, Aunt Rhoda. At Madame Tolmache's they taught us so much geography and geology and astronomy, don't you know, that they were obliged to keep us in the dark about uncles and aunts. And am I really to call the Rector, uncle? It seems quite awful."

"Why awful?"

"Because I have looked up to him all my life as a being in a black silk gown who preached long sermons and would do something awful to me if

I laughed in church. I looked upon him as the very embodiment of the Church, don't you know, and should hardly have believed that he wanted breakfast and dinner, and wore out his clothes and boots like other men. When he came to call I used to run away and hide myself. I had an idea that he would scold me if I came in his way—take me to task for not being a christian, or ask me to repeat last Sunday's Gospel. And to think that he should be my uncle. How curiously things come round in this life!"

"I hope you will not cease to respect him, and that you will learn to love him," said Aunt Rhoda severely.

"Learn to love him! Do you think he would like it?" asked Daphne doubtfully.

"He would like you to behave to him as a niece ought, Daphne. Marmaduke considers my relations his own."

"I'm sure it is very good of him," said Daphne, "but I should think it must come a little difficult after having known us so long in quite another capacity."

The Rector's wife gave her niece a look of half interrogation, half disapproval. She did not know how much malice might lurk under the girl's seeming innocence. She and Daphne had never got on very well together in the old days, when Miss Lawford was the mistress of South Hill, and the arbiter of her nieces' lives.

A year ago, and Rhoda Lawford, at three-and-forty, was still Rhoda Lawford; and any idea of matrimonial promotion which she had once cherished might fairly be supposed to have expired in the cold shade of a neighbourhood where there were very few marriageable men. But Rhoda had begun life as a girl with considerable pretensions. She had never asserted herself or been put forward by her friends as a beauty. The material for that kind of reputation was wanting. But she had been admired and praised for her style, her manner, her complexion, her hair, her hands, her feet, her waist, her shoulders. She was a young lady with good points, and had been admired for her points. People had talked of her as the elegant Miss Lawford: and as, happily, elegance is a quality which time need not

impair, Rhoda had gone on being elegant for five-
and-twenty years. The waist and shoulders, the
hands and feet, had never been out of training for a
quarter of a century. More ephemeral charms had
bloomed and faded; and many a fair friend of
Rhoda's who had triumphed in the insolence of
conscious beauty was now a *passée* matron, of
whom her acquaintance said pityingly, " You have
no idea how pretty that woman was fifteen years
ago;" but the elegant Miss Lawford's attractions
were unimpaired, and the elegant Miss Lawford had
not yet surrendered the hope of winning a prize in
the matrimonial lottery.

The living of Baddesley-with-Arden was one of
those fat sinecures which are usually given to men
of good family and considerable private means.
The Reverend Marmaduke Ferrers was the descendant of a race well rooted in the soil, and had,
by the demise of two bachelor uncles and three
maiden aunts, accumulated to himself a handsome
property, in land, and houses, and the safer kind of
public securities. These legacies had fallen in at
longish intervals, some of the aunts being slow in

relaxing their grip upon this world's gear; but had all the wealth of a Westminster or a Rothschild been poured into the Reverend Marmaduke's lap, he would not have renounced the great tithes of Baddesley-with-Arden, or the important, and, in a manner, judicial and dictatorial position which he held as Rector of those two small parishes. Mr. Ferrers loved the exercise of authority on a small scale. He had an autocratic mind, but it was a very small mind, and it suited him to be the autocrat of two insignificant pastoral villages, rather than to measure his power against the men of cities. To hector Giles for getting drunk on a Saturday night, to lecture Joan for her absence from church on Sunday, afforded the Rector as much delight as a bigger man might have felt in towering over the riot of a Republican chamber or proroguing a Rump parliament. Mr. Ferrers had been Rector of Baddesley thirty years, and in all that time he had never once thought of taking to himself a wife. He had a lovely old Rectory and a lovelier garden; he had the best servants in the neighbourhood—partly because he was a most exacting master, and partly because he paid his housekeeper largely, and made her responsible for everybody else. The whole machinery of his life worked with a delightful smoothness. He had nothing to gain from matrimony in the way of domestic comfort; and there is always the possibility of loss. Thus it happened that although he had gone on admiring Miss Lawford for a round dozen years, talking of her as a most ladylike and remarkably well-informed person, pouring all his small grievances into her ear, confiding to her the most recondite details of any little complaint from which he happened to suffer, consulting her about his garden, his stable, his parish, it had never occurred to him that he should improve his condition or increase his happiness by making the lady his wife.

Yet, throughout this time, Rhoda Lawford had always had it in her mind that if all other views failed, she could wind up fairly well by marrying the Rector. It was not at all the kind of fate she had imagined for herself years ago in the freshness of her charms; but it would be a respectable match. Nobody could presume to pity her, or say that she had done badly. The Rector was ten years her senior, so nobody could laugh at her for marrying a youth. Altogether there would be a fitness and a propriety about the alliance, which would be in perfect harmony with the elegance of her person and the spotlessness of her character. On her fortieth birthday, Miss Lawford told herself that the time had now come when the Rector must be taken seriously in hand, and taught to see what was good for himself. A friendship which had been meandering on for the last twelve years must be brought to a head; dangling attention and old-fashioned compliments must be reduced into something more tangible. In a word, the Rector must be converted from a friend into a suitor.

It had taken Miss Lawford two years to open the Reverend Marmaduke's eyes; but at the end of those two years the thing was done, and the Rector was sighing, somewhat apoplectically, for the approach of his wedding-day, and the privilege of claiming Rhoda for his own. The whole process had been carried out with such consummate tact

that Marmaduke Ferrers had not the faintest
suspicion that the matrimonial card which he had
drawn had been forced upon him. He believed in
his engagement as the spontaneous growth of his
own mind. "Strange that I should have known
you so long, my Rhoda, and only discovered lately
that you were so dear to me," he murmured in his
fat voice, as he dawdled with his betrothed in one
of those shadowy Warwickshire lanes which seem
made for the meanderings of lovers. His Rhoda
smiled tenderly; and then they began to talk about
the new carpet for the Rectory drawing-room, the
Sèvres garniture de cheminée which Sir Vernon had
given his sister for a wedding present, dwelling
rather upon the objective than the subjective
side of their position, as middle-aged lovers are apt
to do.

"I hope you will not mind my keeping Todd,"
said the Rector presently, pausing to recover his
breath, and plucking a dog-rose in absence of
mind.

"Dearest, have I any wish in opposition to

yours ? " murmured Rhoda, but not without a
shadow of sourness in the droop of her lips, for she
had a shrewd idea that so long as the Rector's
housekeeper, Mrs. Todd, remained at the Rectory,
nobody else could be mistress there.

CHAPTER VI.

"LOVE MAKETH ALL TO GONE MISWAY."

AUNT RHODA was not a person to be set at defiance,
even by Daphne, who was by no means a tract-
able spirit. She had said, "Come to the Rectory,"
and had said it with such an air of offended dignity
that Daphne felt she must obey, and promptly,
lest a worse lecture should befall her. So directly
after luncheon on the following day she changed
her gown, and prepared herself for the distasteful
visit. Madoline was going to drive to Warwick
with her father, so Daphne would have to perform
her penance alone.

It was a lovely afternoon in the first week of
May, the air balmy and summer-like, the meadows

looking their greenest before the golden glory of
buttercup time. Yonder in the reedy hollows the
first of the marsh marigolds were opening their
yellow cups, and smiling up at the yellow sun.
The walk to Arden Rectory was something over a
mile, and it was as lovely a walk as anyone need
care to take ; through meadows, beside flowery
hedgerows, with the river flowing near, but almost
hidden by a thick screen of willows ; and then
by one of the most delightful lanes in the county,
a green arcade of old elms, with here a spreading
oak, and there a mountain ash, to give variety to
the foliage.

Daphne set out alone, as soon as she had seen
the carriage drive away from the door ; but she
was not destined to go her way unaccompanied.
Half way down the avenue she met Mr. Turchill,
strolling at a lazy pace, a cigar in his mouth, and
a red setter of Irish pedigree at his heels.

At sight of Daphne he threw away his cigar,
and took his hands out of his pockets.

"I was coming up to the Hill to ask somebody

to play a game of billiards, and everybody seems going out," he said.

They had known him so long in an easy-going neighbourly way that he almost took rank as a relation. Daphne, who had spent so much of her life away from home, had naturally seen less of him than anybody else; but as she had been a child during the greater part of their acquaintance, he had fallen into the way of treating her as an elder brother might have done; and he had not yet become impressed with the dignity of her advancing years. For him she was still the Daphne he had romped with in the Christmas holidays, and whose very small pony it had been his particular care to get broken.

"I met Madoline and Sir Vernon going to Warwick. Why go to Warwick? What is there for anyone but a Cook's tourist to do in Warwick? But I thought you would be at home. You haven't a bad notion of billiards, and you might have helped a fellow to while away an afternoon."

"You are like the idle boy in the spelling-book story, wanting someone to play with you," said

Daphne, laughing at him. He had turned, and was walking beside her, the docile setter following meekly, like a dog who felt that he was of no consequence in the world now that the days of sport were done.

"Well, the hunting's all over, don't you know, and there's no more shooting, and I never cared much for fishing, and I've got such a confoundedly clever bailiff that he won't let me open my mouth on the farm. So the days do hang rather heavy on a fellow's hands."

"Why don't you take to Alpine climbing?" suggested Daphne. "I don't mean Mont Blanc—everybody does that—but the Matterhorn, or Monte Rosa, or something. If I were a young man I should amuse myself in that way."

"I don't set an exaggerated value on my life, but when I do make up my mind to throw it away, I think I'll do the thing more comfortably," replied Edgar Turchill. "Don't trouble yourself to suggest employment for me. I'm not complaining of my life. There's a good deal of loafing in it, but I rather like loafing, especially when I can loaf in pleasant company. Where are you going, and may I go with you?"

"I am going on a duty visit to Aunt Rhoda and my new uncle. Isn't it rather dreadful to have an uncle thrust upon one in that way?"

"Well," returned Edgar deliberately, "I must say if I had the choosing of my relations I should leave out the Rector. But you needn't mind him. Practically he's no more to you than he was before he married your aunt."

"I don't know," said Daphne doubtfully. "He may take liberties. He was always a lecturing old thing, and he'll lecture ever so much more now that he's a relation."

"But you needn't stand his lecturing. Just tell him quietly that you don't hold with clerical interference in the affairs of the laity."

"He got me ready for my confirmation, and that gave him a kind of hold over me," said Daphne. "You see, he found out the depth of my ignorance."

"I'll wager he'd be ploughed in a divinity exam. to-morrow," said Edgar. "These old heathens of village parsons got there degrees in a day when the dons were a set of sleepy-headed old duffers like themselves. But don't let's talk about him. What is Madoline going to do in Warwick?"

"She and my father are going to make some calls in the neighbourhood, and I believe she has a little shopping to do."

"Why didn't you go with them?"

"Papa does not like to have three people in the barouche. Besides, I had promised to call on my aunt. She talked to me quite awfully last night about my want of proper feeling in never having visited her in her new house."

"Why didn't you wait till she asked you to dinner? They give capital dinners at the Rectory, but their feeds are few and far between. I don't want to say anything rude about your aunt, but she strikes me as a lady who has too keen an appreciation of the value of money to fritter it away upon other people."

"Why don't you say at once that she's horribly stingy?" said the outspoken Daphne. "I don't

think she ever spent sixpence, except upon her
own clothes, all the time she lived in my father's
house, and I know she was always getting gowns
and bonnets out of Madoline. I've seen her do it.
But please don't let's talk of her any more. It's
rather worse than talking of him. I shall have to
kiss her, and call her dear aunt, presently, and I
shall detest myself for being such a hypocrite."

They had gone out by the lodge-gate by this
time, the lodge with its thatched roof and dormer
window, like a big eye looking out under a shaggy
pent-house eyebrow; the lodge by which there
grew one of those tall deodaras which were the
chief glory of the grounds at South Hill. They
crossed the high road, and entered the meadow-
path which led towards Arden Rectory; and the
setter finding himself at large in a field, frisked
about a little, as if with a faint suspicion of
partridges.

"Oh, by-the-bye," began Daphne, in quite a
new tone, "now that we are alone, I want you to
tell me all about Lina's engagement. Is he nice?"

Edgar Turchill's face clouded over so darkly

that the look seemed a sufficient answer to her question.

"Oh, I see," she said. "You don't like him."

"I can't say that. He's an old acquaintance —a friend—a kind of family connection even, for his mother's grandmother was a Turchill. But to be candid, I don't like the engagement."

"Why not, unless you know something against him?"

"I know nothing against him. He is a gentleman. He is ten times cleverer than I, ten times richer, a great deal handsomer—my superior in every way. I should be a mean cad if I couldn't acknowledge as much as that. But——"

"You think Lina ought not to have accepted him."

"I think the match in every way suitable, natural, inevitable. How could he help falling in love with her? Why should she refuse him?"

"You are talking in riddles," said Daphne. "You say it is a suitable match, and a minute ago you said you did not like the engagement."

"I say so still. Can't you imagine a reason for my feeling?"

Daphne contemplated him thoughtfully for a few moments as they walked on. His frank English face looked graver than she ever remembered to have seen it—grave to mournfulness.

"I am very sorry," she faltered. "I see. You were fond of her yourself. I am desperately sorry. I should have liked you ever so much better for a brother."

"Don't say that till you have seen Gerald. He has wonderful powers of fascination. He paints and poetises, and all that kind of thing, don't you know; the sort of thing that pleases women. He can't ride a little bit—no seat—no hands."

"How dreadful!" cried Daphne, aghast. "Does he tumble off?"

"I don't mean that. He can stick in his saddle somehow; and he hunts when he's at home in the season; but he can't ride."

"Oh," said Daphne, as if she were trying to understand this distinction.

"Yes, Daphne. I don't mind your knowing it—now it's all over and done with," pursued Edgar, glad to pour his griefs into a friendly ear. "You're my old playfellow—almost like a little sister—and I don't think you'll laugh at me, will you, dear?"

"Laugh at you!" cried Daphne. "If I do may I never be able to smile again."

"I asked your sister to marry me. I had gone on loving her for I don't know how long, before I could pluck up courage to ask the question. I was so afraid of being refused. And I knew if she would only say 'Yes,' that my mother would be the proudest woman in the county, for she positively adores Madoline. And I knew Lina liked Hawks-yard; and that was encouraging. So one day, about four years ago, I got desperate, and asked the plain question in a plain way. Heaven knows how much of my happiness hung on the answer; but I couldn't have screwed any poetry out of myself to save my life. I could only tell her the honest truth—that I loved her as well as man ever loved woman."

" Well ? " asked Daphne.

" It was no use. She said ' No,' so kindly, so sweetly, so affectionately—for she really likes me, you know, in a sisterly way—that she made me cry like a child. Yes, Daphne, I made a miserable ass of myself. She must have despised such unmanly weakness. And then in a few minutes it was all over. All my hopes were extinguished, like a candle blown out by the wind, and all my future life was dark. And I had to go back and tell the poor mother that the daughter she wanted was never to come to Hawksyard."

" I am so sorry for you," faltered Daphne.

" Thank you, dear. I knew you would be sympathetic. The blow was a crusher, I assure you. I went away for a few months deer-stalking in the Highlands; but lying on a mountain side in a gray mist for hours on end, not daring to move an eyelash, gives a fellow too much time for thought. I was always thinking of Madoline, and my thoughts were just two hundred and fifty miles due south of the stag when he came across, so I generally shot wild, and felt myself altogether a failure. Then I tried a month in Normandy and Brittany with a knapsack, thinking I might walk down my trouble. But I found that tramping from one badly-drained town to another badly-drained town—all infected with garlic—and looking at churches I didn't particularly want to see, was a sham kind of consolation for a very real disappointment; so I made up my mind to come back to Hawksyard and live it down. And I have lived it down," concluded Edgar exultantly.

"You don't care for Madoline any longer?"

"Not care for her! I shall worship her as long as I have breath in my body. But I have resigned myself to the idea that somebody else is going to marry her—that the most I can ever be to her is a good, useful, humdrum kind of friend, who will be godfather to one of her boys by-and-by; ready to ride helter-skelter for the doctor if any of her children show symptoms of measles or whooping-cough; glad to take dummy of an evening when she and her husband want to play whist; or to entertain the boys at Hawksyard for their summer holidays while she and he are enjoying a *tête-à-tête* ramble in the Engadine. That is the sort of man I shall be."

"How good you are!" said Daphne, slipping her hand through his arm with an affectionate impulse.

"Ah, my little Daphne, it will be your turn to **fall** in love some of these days; put it off as long as you **can, dear,** for there's more pain than pleasure in it at best." Daphne gave an involuntary sigh. "And then I hope you'll confide **in me** just as freely as I have confided in **you.** I may be useful as an adviser, you **know,** having **had my own** troubles."

"You could only advise me to be patient, and give up all hope," said Daphne, drawing her hand from his arm. "What would be the good of such **advice?** But I shall never trouble you. **I am not** going to **fall** in love—ever."

She gave the last word an almost **angry** emphasis.

"Poor little Daphne! as if you could **know** anything about it," exclaimed Edgar, smiling incredulously at her. "That kind of thing comes upon one unawares. You talk as if you could choose whether you would fall in love or not— like Hercules between his two roads, deliberating whether he should go to the right or the left. Ah, my dear, when we come to that stage of our journey there is but one road for us : and whether it lead to the Garden of Eden or the Slough of Despond, we must travel over it."

"You are getting poetical," exclaimed Daphne scornfully; "I didn't know that was in your line. But please tell me about Gerald. I have never seen him, you know. He was always at Oxford, or roaming about the world somewhere, when I was at home for the holidays. I have been at home so little, you see," she interjected with a piteous air. "I used to hear a great deal about a very wonderful personage, enormously rich, fabulously clever, and accomplished, and hand-some; and I grew rather to hate him, as one is apt to hate such perfection; and then one day I got a letter from Lina—a letter brimming over with happiness—to say that she and this demigod were engaged to be married, but it was to be a

long engagement, because the other demigod—
my father—wished for delay. So you see I know
very little about my future brother."

"You are sure to like him," said Edgar with
a somewhat regretful air. "He has all the qualities
which please women. Another man might be
as handsome, or even handsomer, yet not half so
sure of winning a woman's love. There is something languid, lackadaisical—poetical, I suppose
Madoline would call it—in his appearance and
manner which women admire."

"I hope he is not effeminate," exclaimed
Daphne. "I hate a womanish man."

"No; I don't think anyone could call him
effeminate; but he is dreamy, bookish, fond of
lolling about under trees, smoking cigarettes and
reading verses."

"I'm certain I shall detest him," said Daphne
with conviction, "and it will be very dreadful,
since I must pretend to like him for Lina's sake.
You must stand by me, Edgar, when he is at the
Hill. You and I can chum together, and leave
the lovers to spoon by themselves. Oh, by-

the-bye, of course you haven't lived on the Avon
all your life without being able to row a boat?"

"No; I can row pretty well."

"Then you must teach me, please. I am going
to have a boat, my very own. It is being built
for me. You'll teach me to row, won't you,
Edgar?" she asked with a pleading smile.

"I shall be delighted."

"Thanks tremendously. That will be ever
so much better than learning of Bink."

"Indeed! And who is Bink?" asked Edgar,
somewhat dashed.

"One of the under gardeners. Such an honest
creature, and devoted to me."

"I see; and your first idea was to have been
taught by Bink?"

"If there had been no one else," she admitted
apologetically. "You see, having ordered a boat,
it is essential that I should learn to row."

"Naturally."

They had arrived at the last field by this time.
The village lay before them in the sunlight: an old
gray church in an old churchyard on the edge of

the river, a cluster of half-timbered cottages, with walls of wattle and dab, a homestead dwarfed by rick-yard and barns, and finally the Rectory, a low, many-gabled house, half-timbered, like the cottages, a regular sixteenth-century house, with clustered chimneys of massive ruddy-brown brick-work, finished by a stone coping, in which the martens had built from time immemorial.

"I can't tell you how glad I am to have you with me," said Daphne as they came near the stile. "It will take the edge off my visit."

"Oh, but I did not mean to go in with you. I only walked with you for the pleasure of being your escort."

"Nonsense; you are going in, and you are going to stay till I go home, and you are going back with me to dinner. I'm sure you must owe Aunt Rhoda a call. Just consider now if you don't."

Edgar, who had a guilty memory of being a guest at one of the Rector's rare but admirable dinners, just five weeks ago, blushed as he admitted his indebtedness.

"I certainly haven't called since I dined there," he said; "but the fact is, I don't get on very fast with your aunt, although I've known her so long."

"Of course not. I never knew anyone who could get on with her, except Lina, and she's an angel."

They came to the stile, which was what the country people call a tumble-down stile, all the timbers of the gate sliding down with a clatter when a handle is moved, and leaving space for the pedestrian to step over. The Rectory gate stood before them, a low wide gate, standing open to admit the entrance of a carriage. The garden was lovely, even before the season of bedding-out plants and carpet horticulture. For the last twenty years the Rector had annually imported a choice selection of Dutch bulbs, whereby his flower-beds and borders on this May afternoon were a blaze of colour—tulip, hyacinth, ranunculus, polyanthus—each and every flower that blooms in the sweet youth of the year: and as a background for the level lawn with its many flower-beds, there was a belt of such timber and an inner circle of such shrubs as are only to be found in a garden that has been cultivated and improved for a century or so. Copper beeches, Spanish chestnuts, curious specimens of the oak tribe, the feathery foliage of acacia and mountain ash, the pink bloom of the wild plum, and the snowy clusters of the American crab, deodara, cypress, yew, and in the foreground arbutus and seringa, lilac, laburnum, guelder rose, with all the family of laurel, laurustinus, and bay; a shrubbery so exquisitely kept, that not a blighted branch or withered leaf was to be seen in the spacious circle which fenced and protected that smiling lawn from all the outer world.

The house was, in its way, as perfect as the garden. There were many rooms, but none large or lofty. The Rectory had all the shortcomings and all the fascinations of an old house: wide hearths and dog-stoves, high mantel-pieces, deep recessed casements, diamond panes, leaden lattices, massive roughly - hewn beams supporting the ceilings, a wide shallow staircase, rooms opening one out of another, irregular levels, dark oak floors, a little stained glass here and there—real old glass, of rich dark red, or sombre green, or deep dull topaz.

The house was delightfully furnished, though Mr. Ferrers had never taken any trouble about it. Many a collector, worn out before his time by the fever and anxiety of long summer afternoons at Christie's, would have envied Marmaduke Ferrers the treasures which had fallen to him without the trouble of collecting. Residuary legatee to all his aunts and uncles, he had taken to himself the things that were worth having among their goods and chattels, and had sold all the rubbish.

The aunts and uncles had been old-fashioned non-locomotive people, hoarding up and garnering the furniture of past generations. Thus had the rector acquired Chippendale chairs and tables, old Dutch tulip-wood cabinets and bureaus, Louis Quinze commodes, Elizabethan clocks, Derby and Worcester, Bow, Bristol, Leeds, and Swansea crockery, with a sprinkling of those dubious jugs and bowls that are generally fathered on Lowestoft.

Past generations had amassed and hoarded in order that the Rector might be rich in art treasures without ever putting his hand in his pocket. Furniture that had cost a few pounds when it was bought was now worth hundreds, and the Rector had it all for nothing, just because he came of a selfish celibate race.

The Chippendale furniture, the Dutch marqueterie work, old china, and old plate had all been in Miss Lawford's mind when she took the Rector in hand and brought him to see her fitness for his wife.

True that her home at South Hill was as elegant, and in all things as desirable; but there was a wide difference between living under the roof of her brother, more or less on sufferance, and being mistress of her own house. Thus the humbler charms of the Rectory impressed her more than the dignity of the Hill. Sir Vernon Lawford was not a pleasant man to whom to be beholden. His daughters were now grown up. Madoline was sovereign mistress of the house which must one day be her own; and Rhoda

Lawford felt that to stay at the Hill would be to sink to the humdrum position of a maiden aunt, for whom nobody cared very much.

Mrs. Ferrers was sitting in a Japanese chair on the lawn, in front of the drawing-room windows, nursing a black and white Japanese pug, and rather yearning for someone from the outer world, even in that earthly paradise where the guelder roses were all in bloom and the air was heavy with the odour of hawthorn-blossom.

"At last!" she exclaimed, as Daphne and her companion made their timorous advance across the velvet turf, mown twice a week in the growing season. "You too, Mr. Turchill; I thought you were never coming to see me."

"After that delightful evening with the Mowbrays and the people from Liddington! It was too ungrateful of me," said Edgar. "If you call me Mr. Turchill I shall think I am never to be forgiven."

"Well, then, it shall be Edgar, as it was in the old days," said Mrs. Ferrers, with a faint suspicion of sentiment.

There had been a time when it had seemed to
her not altogether impossible that she should
become Mrs. Turchill. Hawksyard Grange was such
a delicious old place; and Edgar was her junior by
only fourteen years.

"I don't wan't you to make ceremonious calls
just because you happen to have dined here; but
I want you to drop in often because you like us.   I
want you to bring me breathings of the outside world.
The life of a clergyman's wife in a country parish is
so narrow.   I feel hourly becoming a vegetable."

Mrs. Ferrers looked complacently down at her
tea-gown of soft creamy Indian silk, copiously
trimmed with softer Breton lace, and felt that at
least she was a very well-dressed vegetable.   Knots
of palest blue satin nestled here and there among
the lace; a cluster of hot-house roses—large velvety
yellow roses—reposed on Mrs. Ferrers's shoulder,
and agreeably contrasted with her dark, smoothly-
banded hair.   She prided herself on the classic
form of her small head, and the classic simplicity of
her coiffure.

"I think we all belong, more or less, to the

vegetable tribe about here," said Mr. Turchill. "There is something sleepy in the very air of our pastoral valleys. I sometimes long to get away to the stone-wall country yonder, on the Cotswolds, to breathe a freer, more wakeful air."

" I can't say that I languish for the Cotswolds," replied Mrs. Ferrers, " but I should very much like a fortnight in Mayfair. Do you know if your father and Madoline are going to London this season, Daphne ? "

" I think not. Papa fancies himself not quite well enough for the fatigue of London, and Lina does not care about going."

It had been Sir Vernon's habit to take a furnished house at the West End for part of May and June, in order to see all the picture-galleries, and hear all the operas that were worth being heard, and to do a little visiting among his very select circle of acquaintance. He was not a man who made new acquaintances if he could help it, or who went to people because they lived in big houses and gave big dinners. He was exclusive to a fault, detested crowds, and had a rooted

conviction that **every new** man was a swindler,
who was destined to end his career in ignominious
bankruptcy. It had gone hard with him to consent
to his daughter's engagement with a man who on
the father's side was a parvenu; but he had
consoled himself as best he might with the idea of
Lady Geraldine's blue **blood, and** Mr. Goring's
very substantial fortune.

"And so you are no longer a school-girl,
Daphne, **and have come** home for good," said Mrs.
Ferrers, dropping her elegant society manner and
putting on a sententious air, which Daphne knew
too well. "I hope you are going to try to
improve yourself—for what girls learn at school
is a mere smattering—and that you are aware how
much room there is for improvement—in your
carriage, for instance."

"I haven't any carriage, aunt, but papa **is**
going to let me keep a boat," said Daphne, who
had been absently watching **the** little yellow
butterflies skimming **above** the flame-coloured
tulips.

"My dear, **I am** talking of your deportment.

You are sitting most awkwardly at this moment, one shoulder at least three inches higher than the other."

"Don't worry about it, aunt," said Daphne indifferently; "perhaps it's a natural deformity."

"I hope not. I think it rests with yourself to become a very decent figure," replied Mrs. Ferrers, straightening her own slim waist. "Here comes your uncle, returning from his round of duty in time to enjoy his afternoon tea."

The Rector drove up to the gate in a low park-phaeton, drawn by a sleek bay cob; a cob too well fed and lazy to think of running away, but a little apt to become what the groom called "a bit above himself," and to prance and toss his head in an arrogant manner, or even to shy at a stray rabbit, as if he had never seen such a creature before, and hadn't the least idea what the apparition meant. The Rector's round of duty had been a quiet drive through elm-shadowed lanes, and rustic occupation roads, with an occasional pull-up before the door of a cottage, or a farm-house, where, without alighting, he would inquire

in a fat pompous voice after the welfare, spiritual
and temporal, of his parishioners, and then shedding
on them the light of a benignant smile, or a few
solemn words of clerical patronage, he would give
the reins a gentle shake and drive off again. This
kind of parochial visitation, lasting for about two
hours, the Rector performed twice or three times
a week, always selecting a fine afternoon. It kept
him in the fresh air, gave him an appetite for his
dinner, and maintained pleasant relations between
the pastor and his flock.

Mr. Ferrers flung the reins to his groom, a man
of middle age, in sober dark livery, and got himself
ponderously out of his carriage on to the gravel
drive. He was a large man, tall and broad, with
a high bald head, red-brown eyes of the protuberant
order, a florid complexion, pendulous cheeks and
chin, and mutton-chop whiskers of a warm chestnut. He was a man whose appearance, even to the
stranger, suggested a life devoted to dining; a
man to whom dinner was the one abiding reality of
life, the same yesterday, to-day, and to-morrow—
a memory, an actuality, a hope. He was the man

for whom asparagus and peas are forced into untimely perfection—the man who eats poached salmon in January, and gives a fabulous price for the first of the grouse—the man for whom green geese are roasted in June, and who requires immature turkeys to be fatted for him in October; who can enjoy oysters at fourpence a piece; who thinks ninety shillings a dozen a reasonable price for dry champagne, and would drive thirty miles to secure a few dozen of the late Colonel Somebody's famous East India sherry.

Rhoda had married the Reverend Marmaduke with her eyes fully opened to the materialistic side of his character. She knew that if she wanted to live happily with him and to exercise that gentle and imperceptible sway, which vulgar people call hen-pecking, she must make dinner the chief study of her life. So long as she gave full satisfaction upon this point; so long as she could maintain a table, in which the homely English virtue of sub-stantial abundance was combined with the artistic variety of French cooking; so long as she antici-pated the Rector's fancies, and forestalled the seasons, she would be sure to please. But an hour's forgetfulness of his tastes or prejudices, a single failure, an experimental dish, would shatter for the time being the whole fabric of domestic bliss, and weaken her hold of the matrimonial sceptre. The Rector's wife had considered all this before she took upon herself the responsibilities of married life. Supremely indifferent herself to the pleasures of the table, she had to devote one thoughtful hour of every day to the consideration of what her husband would like to eat, drink, and avoid. She had to project her mind into the future to secure for him novelty of diet. Todd, the housekeeper, had ministered to him for many years, and knew all his tastes: but Mrs. Ferrers wanted to do better than Todd had done, and to prove to the Rector that he had acted wisely in committing himself to the dulcet bondage of matrimony. She was a clever woman—not bookish or highly cultured—but skilled in all the small arts and devices of daily life; and so far she had succeeded admirably. The Rector, granted the supreme indulgence of all his desires, was his wife's admiring slave. He flattered her, he deferred to her, he praised her, he boasted of her to all his acquaintance as the most perfect thing in wives, just as he boasted of the sleek bay as the paragon of cobs, and his garden as the archetype of gardens.

And now for the first time Daphne had to salute this great man in his new character of an uncle. She went up to him timidly; a graceful, gracious figure in a pale yellow batiste gown, a knot of straw-coloured Marguerites shining on her breast, her lovely liquid eyes darkened by the shadow of her Tuscan hat.

"How do you do—uncle?" she said, holding out a slender hand, in a long loose Swedish glove.

The Rector started, and stared at her dumbly; whether bewildered by so fair a vision, or taken aback by the unexpected assertion of kinsmanship, only he himself knew.

"Bless my soul;" he cried. "Is this Daphne? Why the child has grown out of all knowledge. How d'ye do, my dear? Very glad to see you.

You'll stop to dinner, of course.   You **and** Turchill.
How d'ye do, Turchill ? ''

The **Rector** had a troublesome trick of asking
everybody who crossed his threshold in the afternoon to dinner.   He had **an abiding idea that** his
friends wanted to be fed ; that **they** would rather
dine with him than go home; and that if **they**
refused, their refusal was mere modesty **and** self-
denial, **and ought not to be accepted.   Vainly had**
Rhoda lectured **her spouse upon this evil habit,**
vainly had she **tried** to demonstrate **to him that an**
afternoon visit should be received as **such,** and need
not degenerate into a dinner-party. The Rector was
incorrigible.   Hospitality was his redeeming virtue.

"Thanks awfully," replied Daphne; "but I
must go **home** to dinner.   Papa and Lina expect
me.   **Of course Mr.** Turchill can do **as he likes.''**

"Then Turchill will stay," said the Rector.

"My dear Rector, **you are very kind, but** I must
go home with Daphne.   I **brought** her, don't you
see, **and I'm bound to take her back.   There might**
be a bull, or something."

"Do you think I am afraid of bulls?" cried Daphne; "why I love the whole cow tribe. If I saw a bull in one of our meadows, I should walk up to him and make friends."

The Rector surveyed the yellow damsel with an unctuous smile.

"It would be dangerous," he said in his fat voice, "if I were the bull."

"Why?"

"I should be tempted to imitate an animal famous in classic story, and swim the Avon with you on my back," replied the Rector.

"Duke," said Mrs. Ferrers with her blandest smile, "don't you think you had better rest yourself in your cool study while we take our tea. I'm sure you must be tired after your long drive. These first warm days are so exhausting. I'll bring you your cup of tea."

"Don't trouble yourself, my love," replied the Rector; "Daphne can wait upon me. Her legs are younger than yours."

This unflattering comparison, to say nothing of the vulgar allusion to "legs," was too much for

Rhoda's carefully educated temper. She gave her Marmaduke a glance of undisguised displeasure.

"I am not so ancient or infirm as to find my duties irksome," she said severely; "I shall certainly bring you your tea."

The Rector had a weakness about pretty girls. There was no harm in it. He had lived all his life in an atmosphere of beauty, and no scandal had ever arisen about peeress or peasant. He happened to possess an artistic appreciation of female loveliness, and he took no trouble to disguise the fact. Youth and beauty and freshness were to him as the very wine of life—second only to actual Cliquot, or Roederer, Clos Vougeot, or Marcobrünner. His wife was too well acquainted with this weakness. She had known it years before she had secured Marmaduke for her own; and she had flattered herself that she could cure him of this inclination to philander; but so far the curative process had been a failure.

But Marmaduke, though inclined to folly, was not rebellious. He loved a gentle doze in the cool shade of his study, where there were old-fashioned easy-chairs of a shape more comfortable than has ever revealed itself to the mind of modern upholsterer. The brief slumber gave him strength to support the fatigue of dressing for dinner, for the Reverend Marmaduke was as careful of the outward man as of the inner, and had never been seen in slovenly attire, or with unshaven visage.

Mrs. Ferrers sank into her chair with a sigh of relief as the Rector disappeared through the deep rustic porch. The irreproachable butler, who had grown gray in Mr. Ferrers's service, brought the tea-tray, with its Japanese cups and saucers. Edgar Turchill subsided upon a low rustic stool at Daphne's feet, just where his length of arm would enable him to wait upon the two ladies. They made a pretty domestic group : the westering sun shining upon them, the Japanese pug fawning at their feet, flowers and foliage surrounding them, birds singing, bees humming, cattle lowing in the neighbouring fields.

Edgar looked up admiringly at the bright young face above him: eyes so darkly luminous, a complexion of lilies and roses, that exquisite creamy whiteness

which goes with pale auburn hair, that lovely
varying bloom which seems a beauty of the mind
rather than of the person, so subtly does it indicate
every emotion and follow the phases of thought.
Yes; the face was full of charm, though it was not
the face of his dreams—not the face he had
worshipped for years before he presumed to reveal
his love for the owner. If a man cannot win the
woman he loves it were better surely that he should
teach himself to love one who seems more easily
attainable. The bright particular star shines afar
off in an inaccessible heaven; but lovely humanity
is here at his side, smiling on him, ready to be
wooed and won.

Edgar's reflections did not go quite so far as
this, but he felt that he was spending his afternoon
pleasantly, and he looked forward with complacency
to the homeward walk through the meadows.

CHAPTER VII.

"HIS HERTE BATHED IN A BATH OF BLISSE."

DAPHNE'S boat came home from the builder's at the end of three weeks of longing and expectation, a light wherry-shaped boat, not the tub-like sea-going dingey, but a neat little craft which would have done no discredit to a Thames waterman. Daphne was in raptures; Mr. Turchill was impressed into her service, in nowise reluctant; and all the mornings of that happy June were devoted to the art of rowing a pair of sculls on the rapid Avon. Never had the river been in better condition; there was plenty of water, but there had been no heavy rains since April, and the river had not overflowed its natural limits; the stream ran smoothly between its green and willowy banks, just such a lenient tide as Horace loved to sing.

When Daphne took up a new thing it was a passion with her. She was at the exuberant age when all fresh fancies are fevers. She had had her fever for water-colours, for battledore and shuttlecock, for crewel-work. She had risen at daybreak to pursue each new delight: but this fancy for the boat was the most intense of all her fevers, for the love of the river was a love dating from infancy, and she had never been able to gratify it thoroughly until now. Every evening in the billiard-room she addressed the same prayer to Edgar Turchill, when she bade him good-night: "Come as early as you can to-morrow morning, please." And to do her pleasure the Squire of Hawksyard rose at cockcrow and rode six miles in the dewy morning, so as to be at the boat-house in Sir Vernon's meadow before Arden church clock struck seven.

Let him be there as early as he might Daphne was always waiting for him, fresh as the morning, in her dark blue linen gown and sailor hat, the sleeves tucked up to the elbow to give free play to her supple wrists, her arms lily-white in spite of wind and weather.

"It's much too good of you," said she, in her careless way, not ungrateful, but with the air of a girl who thinks men were created to wait upon her. "How very early you must have been up!"

"Not so much earlier than you. It is only an hour's ride from Hawksyard, even when I take it gently."

"And you have had no breakfast, I daresay."

"I have had nothing since the tumbler of St. Galmier you poured out for me in the billiard-room last night."

"Poor—dear—soul!" sighed Daphne, with a pause after each word. "How quite too shocking! We must institute a gipsy tea-kettle. This kind of thing shall not occur again."

She looked at him with her loveliest smile, as much as to say: "I have made you my slave, but I mean your bondage to be pleasant."

When he came to the boat-house next morning he found a kettle singing gaily on a rakish-looking gipsy-stove, a table laid for breakfast inside the boat-house, a smoking dish of eggs and bacon, and the faithful Bink doing butler, rough and rustic, but devoted.

" I wonder whether she has read Don Juan ? " thought Edgar. The water, the gipsy breakfast, the sweet face smiling at him, reminded him of an episode in that poem. " Were I shipwrecked to-morrow I would not wish to awaken in a fairer paradise," he said to himself, while Bink adjusted a camp-stool for him, breathing his hardest all the time. " This is a delicious surprise," he exclaimed.

" The eggs and bacon ? "

" No; the privilege of a *tête-à-tête* breakfast with you."

" Tête-à-fiddlestick; Bink is my chaperon. If you are impertinent I will ask Mr. MacCloskie to join us to-morrow morning. Sugar ? Yes, of course, sugar and cream. Aren't the eggs and bacon nice ? I cooked them. It was Bink's suggestion. I was going to confine myself to rolls and strawberry jam; but the eggs and bacon are more fun, aren't they? You should have heard how they frizzled and sputtered in the frying-pan. I had no idea bacon was so noisy."

"Your first lesson in cookery," said Edgar. "We shall hear of you graduating at South Kensington."

"My first lesson, indeed! Why, I fried pancakes over a spirit-lamp ever so many times at Asnières; and I don't know which smelt nastiest, the pancakes or the lamp. Our dormitory got into awful disgrace about it."

She had seated herself on her camp-stool and was drinking tea, while she watched Edgar eat the eggs and bacon with an artistic interest in the process.

"Is the bacon done?" she asked. "Did I frizzle it long enough?"

"It's simply delicious; I never ate such a breakfast."

It was indeed a meal in fairyland. The soft clear morning light, the fresh yet balmy atmosphere, the sunlit river and shadowy boat-house, all things about and around lent their enchantment to the scene. Edgar forgot that he had ever cared for anyone in the world except this girl, with the soft gray eyes and sunny hair, and all too captivating smile. To be with her, to watch her, to enjoy her girlishness and bright vivacity, to minister to her amusement and wait upon her fancies—what better use could a young man, free to take his pleasure where he liked, find for his life? And far away in the future, in the remoteness of years to come, Edgar Turchill saw this lovely being, tamed and sobered and subdued into the pattern of his ideal wife, losing no charm that made her girlhood lovely, but gaining the holier graces of womanhood and wifehood. To-day she was little more than a child, seeking her pleasure as a child does, draining the cup of each new joy like a child; and he knew that he was no more to her than the agreeable companion of her pleasures. But such an association, such girlish friendship so freely given, must surely ripen into a warmer feeling.

His pulses could not be so deeply stirred and hers give no responsive throb. There must be some sympathy, some answering emotion in a nature so intensely sensitive.

Cheered by such hopeful reflections, Mr. Turchill ate an excellent breakfast, while Daphne somewhat timorously tried an egg, and was agreeably surprised to find it tasted pretty much the same as if the cook had fried it; a little leathery, perhaps, but that was a detail.

"1 feel so relieved," she said. "I shouldn't have been surprised if I had turned them into chickens. And now, if you have quite finished we'll begin our rowing. I have a conviction that if I don't learn to feather properly to-day I shall never accomplish it while I live."

The boat was ready for them, moored to a steep flight of steps which Bink had hewn out of the bank after his working hours. He had found odd planks in the wood-house, and had contrived to face the steps with timber in a most respectable manner, rewarded by Daphne by sweet words and sweeter looks, and by such a shower of shillings that he had opened a post-office savings-bank book on the strength of her bounty, and felt himself on the road to fortune.

There was the boat in all the smartness of new varnished wood. Daphne had given up her idea of a Pompeian red dado to oblige the boat-builder. There were the oars and sculls, with Daphne's monogram in dark blue and gold; and there, glittering in the sunlight, was the name she had chosen for her craft, in bright golden letters—Nero.

" What a queer name to choose !" said Edgar. " He was such an out-and-out beast, you know."

" Not a bit of it," retorted Daphne. " I read an article yesterday in an old volume of Cornhill, in which the writer demonstrates that he was rather a nice man. He didn't poison Britannicus; he didn't make away with his mamma; he didn't set fire to Rome, though he did play the violin beautifully. He was a very accomplished young man, and the historians of his time were silly gobe - mouches, who jotted down every ridiculous scandal that was floating in society. I think that

Taci—— what's his name ought to be ashamed of himself."

"Oh, Nero has been set on his legs, has he?" said Edgar carelessly, as he took the rudder-lines, while Daphne bent over her sculls, and began —rather too vehemently— to feather. "And I suppose Tiberius was a very meritorious monarch, and all those scandals about Capri were so many airy fictions? Well, it doesn't make much difference to us, does it?—except that it will go hard with me by-and-by, when my boys come to learn the history of the future, to have the young scamps tell me that all I learnt at Rugby was bosh."

"At Rugby!" cried Daphne, suddenly earnest. "You were at Rugby with my brother, weren't you? Were you great friends?"

Edgar leant over the boat, concerned about some weeds that were possibly interfering with the rudder.

"We didn't see much of each other. He was ever so much younger than I, you know."

"Was he nice? Were people fond of him?"

"Everybody was dreadfully sorry when he died of scarlet fever, poor fellow!" answered Edgar, without looking at her.

"Yes, it was terrible, was it not? I can just remember him. Such a bright, handsome boy; full of life and spirits. He used to tease me a good deal, but that is the nature of boys. And then, when I was at Brighton, there came a letter to say that he was dead, and I had to wear black frocks for ever so long. Poor Loftus! How dearly I should have loved him if he had lived!"

"Yes; it would have been nice for you to have a brother, would it not?" said Edgar, still with a shade of embarrassment.

"Nice! It would have been my salvation, to have some one of my own kindred, quite my brother. I love Madoline, with all my heart and soul; but she is only my half-sister. I always feel that there is a difference between us. She is my superior; she comes of a better stock. Nobody ever talks of my mother, or my mother's family; but Lina's parentage is in everybody's mouth; she seems to be related — at least in heraldry — to everybody worth knowing in the county. But Loftus would have been the same clay that I am made of, don't you know, neither better nor worse. Blood is thicker than water."

"That's a morbid feeling of yours, Daphne."

"Is it? I'm afraid I have a few morbid feelings."

"Get rid of them. There never was a better sister than Madoline is to you."

"I know it. She is perfection; but that only makes her further away from me. I reverence her, I look up to her and admire her; but I can never feel on an equality with her."

"That shows your good sense. It is an advantage for you to have someone to look up to."

"Yes; but I should like someone on my own level as well."

"You've got me," said Edgar, bluntly.

"Can't you make a brother of me, for the nonce?"

"For ever and always, if you like," replied Daphne. "I'm sure I've got the best of the bargain. I don't believe any brother would get up at five o'clock to teach me to row."

Edgar felt very sure that Loftus would not have done it; that short-lived youth having been the very essence of selfishness, and debased by a marked inclination towards juvenile profligacy.

"Brothers are not the most self-sacrificing of human beings," he said. "I think you'll find finer instances of devotion in an Irish or a Scottish foster-brother than in the Saxon blood-relation. But Madoline is a sister in a thousand. Take care of that willow," as the boat shot under the drooping foliage of an ancient pollard. "How bright and happy she looked last night!"

"Yes; she had just received a long letter from Gerald, and he talks of coming home sooner than she expected him. He will give up his

fishing in Norway, though I believe he had engaged
an inland sea all to himself, and he will be home
before the end of July. Isn't it nice? I am
dying with curiosity to see what he is like."

" Didn't I describe him to you ? "

" In the vaguest way. You said I was sure
to like him. Now I have an invincible conviction that I shall detest him ; just because it is
my duty to feel a sisterly affection for him."

"Take care that you keep within the line
of duty, and that your affection doesn't go
beyond the sisterly limit," said Edgar, with
a grim smile. " There is no fear of the other
thing."

" What a savage look ! " cried Daphne, laughingly. " How horridly jealous you must be of
him ! "

" Hasn't he robbed me of my first love ? "
demanded Edgar ; " and now——"

" Don't be so gloomy. Didn't you tell me
you had got over your disappointment, and that
you meant to be a dear useful bachelor-uncle to
Madoline's children by-and-by."

"I don't know about being always a bachelor," said Edgar doubtfully. "That would imply that I hadn't got over my disappointment."

"That is what you said the other day. I am only quoting yourself against yourself. I like to think of you as a perpetual bachelor for Lina's sake. It is a more poetical idea than the notion of your consoling yourself with somebody else."

"Yet a man does generally console himself. It is in human nature."

"Don't say another word," cried Daphne. "You are positively hateful this morning — so low and material. I'm afraid it must be the consequence of eggs and bacon, such a vulgar unæsthetic breakfast — Bink's idea. I shall give you bread and butter and strawberries to-morrow, if MacCloskie will let me have any strawberries."

"If you were to talk a little less and row a little more, I think we should get on faster," suggested Edgar, smiling at her.

They had got into a spot where a little green peninsula jutted out into the stream, and where

the current was almost a whirlpool. The boat had
been travelling in a circle for the last five minutes,
while Daphne plied her sculls, unconscious of the
fact. They were nearing Stratford; the low, level
meadows lay round them, the tall spire rose yonder,
above the many-arched Gothic bridge built by good
Sir Hugh Clopton before Shakespeare was born.
William Shakespeare must have crossed it many and
many a time, with the light foot of boyhood; a joyous
spirit, finding ineffable delight in simplest things.
And, again, after he had lived his life and had
measured himself amidst the greatest minds of his
age, in the greatest city of the world, and had
toiled, and conquered independence and fame, and
came back rich enough to buy the great house
hard by the grammar-school, how often must he
have lounged against the gray stone parapet, in
the calm eventide, watching the light linger and
fade upon the reedy river, bats and swallows
skimming across the water, the grand old Gothic
church embowered in trees, and the level meadows
beyond!

They were in the very heart of Shakespeare's

country. Yonder, far away to their right, lay the meadow-path by which he walked to Shottery. Memories of him were interwoven with every feature in the landscape.

"My father told me I was not to go beyond our own meadows," said Daphne, "but of course he meant when I was alone. It is quite different when you are with me."

"Naturally. I think I am capable of taking care of you."

This kind of thing went on for another week of weather which at worst was showery. They breakfasted in the boat-house every morning, Daphne exercising all her ingenuity in the arrangement of the meal, and making rapid strides in the art of cookery.

It must be confessed that Mr. Turchill seemed to enjoy the breakfasts suggested by the vulgar-minded Bink, rather more than those which were direct emanations of Daphne's delicate fancy. He liked broiled mackerel better than cream and raspberry jam. He preferred devilled kidneys to honeycomb and milk-rolls. But whatever Daphne set before him he ate with thankfulness. It was so sweet to spend his mornings in this bright, joyous company. It was a grand thing to have so intelligent a pupil, for Daphne was becoming very skilful in the management of her boat. She was able to navigate her bark safely through the most difficult bits of the deep swift river. She could shoot the narrow arches of Stratford bridge in as good style as a professional waterman.

But when two young pure-minded people are enjoying themselves in this frank, easy-going fashion, there is generally someone of mature age near at hand to suggest evil, and to put a stop to their enjoyment. So it was in this case. The Rector's wife heard of her niece's watery meanderings and gipsy breakfasts, and took upon herself to interfere. Mr. MacCloskie, who had reluctantly furnished a dish of forced strawberries for the boat-house breakfast, happened to stroll over to Arden Rectory in the afternoon with a basket of the same fruit, as an offering from himself to Mrs. Ferrers—an inevitable half-crown tip to the head gardener, and dear at the price in the lady's opinion. Naturally a man of MacCloskie's consequence required refreshment after his walk; so Mrs. Todd entertained him in her snug little sanctum next the pantry, with a dish of strong tea and a crusty knob of homebaked bread, lavishly buttered. Whereupon, in the course of conversation, Mr. MacCloskie let fall that Miss Daphne was carrying on finely with Mr. Turchill, of Hawksyard, and that he supposed that would be a match some of these days. Pressed for details, he described the early breakfasts at the boat-house, the long mornings spent on the river, the afternoons at billiards, the tea-drinkings in the conservatory. All this Todd, who was an irrepressible gossip, retailed to her mistress next morning, when the bill of fare had been written, and the campaign of gluttony for the next twenty-four hours had been carefully mapped out.

Mrs. Ferrers heard with the air of profound indifference which she always assumed on such occasions.

"MacCloskie is an incorrigible gossip," she said, "and you are almost as bad."

But, directly she had dismissed Todd, the fair
Rhoda went up to her dressing-room and arrayed
herself for a rural walk.   Life in a pastoral district,
with a husband of few ideas, will now and then
wax monotonous, and Rhoda was glad to have
some little mental excitement—something which
made it necessary for her to bestir herself, and
which enabled her to be useful, after her manner,
to her kith and kin.

"I shall not speak to her father, yet," she
said to herself.   "He has strict ideas of propriety and might be too severe.   Madoline must
remonstrate with her."

She walked across the smiling fields, light of
foot, buoyed up by the pleasing idea that she was
performing a christian duty, that her errand was
in all things befitting her double position as near
relation and pastor's wife.   She felt that if Fate
had made her a man she would have been an
excellent bishop.   All the sterner duties of that
high calling—visitations, remonstrances, suspensions
—would have come easy to her.

She found Madoline in the morning-room, the

French windows wide open, the balcony full of
flowers, the tables and mantel-piece and cabinets
all abloom with roses.

"Sorry to interrupt your morning practice,
dearest," said Mrs. Ferrers as Madoline rose from
the piano. "You play those sweet classic bits so
deliciously. Mendelssohn, is it not?"

"No; Raff. How early you are, Aunt Rhoda!"

"I have something very particular to say to you,
Lina, so I came directly I had done with Todd."

This kind of address from a woman of Rhoda's
type generally forbodes unpleasantness. Madoline
looked alarmed.

"There's nothing wrong, I hope," she faltered.

"Not absolutely—not intentionally wrong, I
trust," said Mrs. Ferrers. "But it must be put a
stop to immediately."

Madoline turned pale. In the days that were
gone Aunt Rhoda had always been a dreadful
nuisance to the servants. She had been perpetually
making unpleasant discoveries—peculations, dis-
sipations, and carryings-on of divers kinds. Not
unfrequently she had stumbled upon mares'-nests,

and after making everybody uncomfortable for a week or two, had been constrained to confess herself mistaken. Her rule at South Hill had not been peace. And now Lina feared that, even outside the house, Aunt Rhoda had contrived to make one of her terrible discoveries. Someone had been giving away the milk or selling the corn, or stealing garden-stuff.

" What is it, Aunt Rhoda ? "

Mrs. Ferrers did not give a direct answer. Her cold gray eyes made the circuit of the room, and then she asked :

" Where is Daphne ? "

" In her own room—lying down, I think, tired out with rowing."

" And where is Mr. Turchill ? "

" Gone home. He had some important business, I believe—a horse to look at."

" Oh, he does go home sometimes ? "

" How curiously you talk, Aunt Rhoda. Is there any harm in his coming here as often as he likes ? He is our oldest friend. Papa treats him like a son."

"Oh, no harm, of course, if Vernon is satisfied. But I don't wonder Daphne is tired, and is lying down at mid-day—a horribly lazy, unladylike habit, by-the-way. Are you aware that she is down at the boat-house before seven every morning?"

"Certainly, aunt. It is much nicer for her to row at that early hour than later in the day. Edgar is teaching her; she is quite safe in his care."

"And do you know that there is a gipsy breakfast every morning in the boat-house?"

"I have heard something about a tea-kettle, and ham and eggs. Daphne has an idea that she is learning to cook."

"And do you approve of all this?"

Madoline smiled at the question.

"I like her to be happy. I think she wastes a good deal of time; that she is doing nothing to carry on her education; but idleness is only natural in a girl of her age, and she has been at home such a short time, and she is so fond of the river."

"Has it never occurred to you, Madoline, that there is some impropriety in these *tête-à-tête* mornings with Edgar Turchill?"

"Impropriety! Impropriety in Daphne being on friendly terms with Edgar—Edgar, who has been brought up with us almost as a brother!"

"With you, perhaps; not with Daphne. She has spent most of her life away from South Hill. She is little more than a stranger to Mr. Turchill."

"She would be very much surprised if you were to tell her so, and so would Edgar. Why, he used always to make himself her playfellow in her holidays, before she went to Madame Tolmache."

"That was all very well while she was in short frocks. But she is now a woman, and people will talk about her."

"About Daphne, my innocent child-like sister, little more than a child in years, quite a child in gaiety and light-heartedness! How can such an idea enter your head, Aunt Rhoda? Surely the most hardened scandalmonger could not find anything to say against Daphne."

"My dear Madoline," began Mrs. Ferrers severely, "you are usually so sensible in all you do and say that I really wonder at the way you are talking this morning. There are certain rules of conduct, established time out of mind, for well-bred young women; and Daphne can no more violate those rules with impunity than anybody else can. It is not because she wears her hair down her back and her petticoats immodestly scanty that she is to go scot-free," added Aunt Rhoda in a little involuntary burst of malevolence.

She had not been fond of Daphne as a child; she liked her much less as a young woman. To a well-preserved woman of forty, who still affects to be young, there is apt to be something aggravating in the wild freshness and unconscious insolence of lovely seventeen.

"Aunt Rhoda, I think you forget that Daphne is my sister—my very dear sister."

"Your half-sister, Madoline. I forget nothing. It is you who forget that there are reasons in Daphne's antecedents why we should be most especially careful about her."

"It is unkind of you to speak of that, aunt," protested Madoline, blushing. "As to Edgar Turchill, he is my father's favourite companion; he is devoted to all of us. There can be no possible harm in his being a kind of adopted brother to Daphne."

"He was an adopted brother to you three years ago, and we all know what came of it."

"Pshaw! That was a foolish fancy, and is all over and done with."

"The same thing may happen in Daphne's case."

"If it should, would you be sorry? I am sure I should not. I know my father would approve."

"Oh, if Vernon is satisfied with the state of affairs, I can have nothing further to say," replied Mrs. Ferrers with dignity; "but if Daphne were my daughter—and Heaven forbid I should ever have such a responsibility as an overgrown girl of that temperament!—I would allow no boat-house breakfastings, no meanderings on the Avon. However, it is no business of mine," concluded Mrs. Ferrers with an injured air, having said all she

had to say. "How is your water-lily counterpane
getting on?"

"Nearly finished," answered Madoline, delighted
to change the conversation. "It will be ready for
papa's birthday."

"How is my brother, by-the-bye?"

"He has been complaining of rheumatic pains.
I'm afraid we shall have to spend next winter
abroad."

"What nonsense, Lina! It is mere hypochondria
on Vernon's part. He was always full of fancies.
He is as well as I am."

"He does not think so himself, aunt; and he
ought to know best."

"I am not sure of that. A hypochondriac
may fancy he has hydrophobia, but he is not
obliged to be right. You foster Vernon's imagi-
nary complaints by pretending to believe in
them."

Lina did not argue the point, preceiving very
plainly that her aunt was out of temper. Nor did
she press that lady to stay to luncheon, nor offer
any polite impediment to her departure. But the

interference of starched propriety had the usual
effect.   Lightly as Madoline had seemed to hold
her aunt's advice, she was too thorough a woman
not to act upon it.   She went up to Daphne's room
directly Mrs. Ferrers left the house.   She stole
softly in, so as not to disturb the girl's slumber,
and seated herself by the open window calmly to
await her waking.   Daphne's room was one of the
prettiest in the house.   It had a wide window,
overlooking the pastoral valley and winding
Avon.   It was neatly furnished with birch-
wood, and turquoise cretonne, and white and
gold crockery, but it was sorely out of order.
Daphne's gowns of yesterday and the day before
were flung on the sofa.   Daphne's hats of all
the week round were strewed on tables and
chairs.   Her sunshade lay across the dressing-table
among the brushes, and scent bottles, and flower-
glasses, and pincushions, and trumpery.   She had
no maid of her own, and her sister's maid, in whose
articles of service it was to attend upon her, had
renounced that duty as a task impossible of performance.   No well-drilled maid could have any-

thing to do—except when positively obliged—with such an untidy and unpunctual young lady. A young lady who would appoint to have her hair dressed and her gown laced at seven, and come running into the house breathless and panting at twenty minutes to eight; a young lady who made hay of her cuffs and collars whenever she was in a hurry, and whose drawer of ribbons was always being upheaved as if by an earthquake. Daphne, being remonstrated with and complained of, protested that she would infinitely rather wait upon herself than be worried.

"You are all goodness, Lina, dear, but half a maid is no maid. I would rather do without one altogether," she said.

The room was not absolutely ugly, even in its disorder. All the things that were scattered about were pretty things. There were a good many ornaments, such as are apt to be accumulated by young ladies with plenty of pocket-money, and very little common sense. Mock Venetian-glass flower-vases of every shape and colour; Japanese cups and saucers, and fans and screens; Swiss brackets; willow-pattern plates; a jumble of everything trumpery and fashionable; flowers everywhere, and the atmosphere sickly sweet with the odour of tuberose.

Daphne stirred in her sleep, faintly conscious of a new presence in the room, sighed, turned on her pillow, and presently sat up, flushed and towzled, in her indigo gown, just as she had come in from her boating excursion.

"Have you had a nice nap, dear?"

"Lovely. I was awfully tired. We rowed to Stratford Weir."

"And you are quite able to row now?"

"Edgar says I scull as well he does."

"Then, dearest, I think you ought to dispense with Edgar in future and keep to our own meadows, as papa said he wished you to do."

"Oh!" said Daphne. "Is that a message from my father?"

"No, dear. But I am sure it will be better for you to consider his wishes upon this point. He is very particular about being obeyed."

"Oh! very well, Lina. Of course if you wish

it I will tell Edgar the course of lessons is concluded. He has been awfully good. It will be
rather slow without him. **But** I was beginning
to find the breakfasts a weight on my mind. It
was so difficult to maintain variety—and Bink has
such low ideas. Do you **know** that he actually
suggested sausages—pork-sausages in June ! **And**
I could not make him comprehend the nauseous-
ness of the notion."

"**Then** it is understood, darling, that you row
by yourself in future. I know my father would
prefer it."

"You prefer it, Lina; that is enough for me,"
answered Daphne in her coaxing way. "But I
think I ought to give Edgar some little present
for all his goodness to me. A smoking-cap, or a
cigar-case, or an antimacassar for his mother. I
could work it in crewels, don't you know."

"You never finish anything, Daphne."

"Because the beginning is always so much
nicer. But if I should break down in this, you
would finish it, wouldn't you, Lina ?"

"With pleasure, my pet."

Edgar was told that evening that his services as a teacher of rowing would no longer be required. And though the fact was imparted to him with infinite sweetness, he felt as if half the sunshine was taken out of his life.

CHAPTER VIII.

"GOD WOTE THAT WORLDLY JOY IS SONE AGO."

PERFECT mistress of her boat, Daphne revelled in
the lonely delight of the river. She felt no grief
at the loss of Mr. Turchill's company. He had
been very kind to her, he had been altogether
devoted and unselfish, and the gipsy breakfasts in
the old boat-house had been capital fun. But these
delights would have palled in time; while the
languid pleasure of drifting quietly down the
stream, thinking her own thoughts, dreaming her
own dreams, could never know satiety. She was
so full of thoughts, sweet thoughts, vague fancies,
visions of an impossible future, dreams which made
up half her life. What did it matter that this airy

fantastic castle she had built for herself was no earthly edifice, that she could never live in it, or be any nearer it that she was to-day? To her the thing existed, were it only in dreamland; it was a part of herself and of her life; it was of more consequence to her than the common-place routine of daily existence—the dressing, and dining, and driving, and visiting.

Had her life been more varied, full of duty, or even diversified by the frivolous activity of pleasure, she could not have thus given herself up to dreaming. But she had few pleasures and no duties. Madoline held her absolved from every care and every trouble on the ground of her youth. She did not like parish work of any kind; she hated the idea of visiting the poor; so Madoline held her excused from that duty, as from all others. Her mind would awaken to the serious side of life when she was older, her sister thought. She seemed now to belong to the flowers and butterflies, and the fair ephemeral things of the garden.

Thus Daphne, ignored by her father, indulged by her sister, enjoyed a freedom which is rarely

accorded to a girl of seventeen. Her Aunt Rhoda
looked on and disapproved, and hoped piously that
she would come to no harm, and was surprised at
Lina's weakness, and thought Daphne's bright
little boat a blot upon the landscape when it came
gliding down the river below the Rectory windows.
The parson's rich glebe was conterminous with
Sir Vernon Lawford's property, and Daphne hardly
knew where her father's fields ended or where the
church fields began.

Edgar Turchill, degraded from his post of
instructor, still contrived to spend a considerable
portion of his life at South Hill. If he was not
there for lawn-tennis in the afternoon, with the
Rector's wife for a fourth, he was there in the
evening for billiards. He fetched and carried for
Madoline, rode over to Warwick to get her a new
book, or to Leamington to match a skein of crewel.
There was no commission too petty for him, no
office too trivial or lowly, so that he might be
permitted to spend his time with the sisters.

Daphne thought this devotedness a bad sign,
and began to fear that the canker was at his heart,

Q 2

and that he would die for love of Madoline when the fortunate Gerald came home to claim her.

"You poor creature," she said to him one day, "you foolish moth, why flutter round the flame that must destroy you? I declare you are getting worse every day."

"You are wrong," said Edgar; "I believe I am getting cured."

What did Daphne dream about in those languid summer mornings, as her boat moved slowly down the stream in the cool shadow of the willows, with only a gentle dip of the sculls now and then to keep her straight? Her thoughts were all of the past, her fancies were all of the future. Her thoughts were of the nameless stranger who went across the Jura last year—one little year ago— almost at this season. Her dreams were of meeting him again. Yet the chances against such a meeting reduced it almost to an impossibility.

"The world is so horribly large," she reflected sadly, "and I told him such atrocious stories. It will be a just punishment if I never see him any

more. Yet how **am** I to live through my **life**
without ever looking on his face again ! "

It had gone so **far as** this : it seemed to her
almost an absolute need of her soul that they two
should meet, and know more of each other.

The ardent sensitive nature had been **thus**
deeply impressed by the first bright and picturesque
image presented to the girlish fancy. **It was** something more than love **at first sight.** **It was the**
awakening of a fresh young mind to the passion
of love. She had changed from a child **to a**
woman, in the hour when **she met the unknown in**
the forest.

" Who **is he ? what is he ?** where shall I find
him ? " she asked herself. " **He is** the only man I
can ever love. He is the only man I will ever marry.
All other men are low and commonplace **beside**
him."

The river was the confidant and companion **of**
all her dreams—the sweet lonely river, flowing
serenely between green pastures, where the cattle
stood in tranquil idleness, pastern deep in purple

clover. She had no other ear in which to whisper her secret. She had tried, ever so many times, to tell Madoline, and had failed. Lina was so sensible, and would be deeply shocked at such folly. How could she tell Lina—whose wooing had been conducted in the most conventionally correct manner, with everybody's consent and approval—that she had flung her heart under the feet of a nameless stranger, of whom the only one fact she knew was that he was engaged to be married?

So she kept this one foolish secret locked in her own breast. The passion was not deep enough to make her miserable, or to spoil the unsophisticated joys of her life. Perhaps it was rather fancy than passion. It was fed and fostered by all her dreams. But her life was in no wise unhappy because this love lacked more substantial food than dreaming. God had given her that intense delight in Nature, that love of His beautiful earth, for which Faustus thanked his Creator. Field, streamlet, wood, and garden, were sources of inexhaustible pleasure. She loved animals of all kinds. The gray Jersey cows in the marshy water meadows;

the house dogs, and yard dogs, and stable terriers
—supposed to be tremendous at rats, yet never
causing any perceptible diminution of that prolific
race ; the big white horses at the farm, with their
coarse plebeian tails tied up into tight knots, their
manes elaborately plaited, and their harness
bedizened with much brazen ornamentation ;
Madoline's exquisite pair of dark chestnuts,
thoroughbred to the tips of their delicate ears ;
Sir Vernon's massive roadster ; Boiler and Crock,
the old carriage-horses—Daphne had an affection
for them all. They were living things, with soft
friendly eyes, more unvaryingly kind than human
eyes, and they all seemed to love her. She
was more at her ease with them than in the
dimly-lighted, flower-scented drawing-room, where
Sir Vernon always seemed to look at her as if he
wished her away, and where her aunt worried her
about her want of deportment.

With Lina she was always happy. Lina's love
and gentleness never varied.

Daphne came home after a morning wasted on
the river, to sit at her sister's feet while she worked,

or to lie on the sofa while Lina read to her, glad
to get in the thin edge of the educational wedge
in the form of an interesting article from one of
the Quarterlies, or a few pages of good poetry.
Daphne was a fervent lover of verse, so that it
came within the limits of her comprehension.   Her
tastes were catholic; she worshipped Shakespeare;
she adored Byron and Shelley and Tennyson, Mrs.
Browning, and the simpler poems of Robert
Browning; and she had heard vaguely of verses
written by a poet called Swinburne; but this was
all she had been permitted to learn of the latest
development of the lyric muse.   Byron and
Tennyson, it is needless to say, were her especial
favourites.

"One makes me feel wicked, and the other
makes me feel good; but I adore them both," she
said.

"I don't see what you can find in Childe
Harold to make you wicked," argued Madoline,
who had the old-fashioned idea, hereditary of
course, that Byron was the poet of the century.

"Oh, I can hardly tell you; but there is a

something, a sense of shortcoming in the world generally, an idea that life is not worth living, that amidst all that is most beautiful and sacred and solemn and interesting upon earth, one might just as well be dead; one would be better off than walking about a world in which virtue was never rightly rewarded, truth and honour and courage or lofty thoughts never fairly understood—where everything is at sixes and sevens, in short. I know I express myself horribly, but the feeling is difficult to explain."

"I think what you mean is that Byron, even at his loftiest and best, wrote like a misanthrope."

"I suppose that's it. Now, Tennyson, though his poetry never lifts me to the skies, makes me feel that earth is a good place and heaven better; that high thoughts and noble deeds bear their fruit somehow, and somewhere; that it is better to suffer a good deal, and sacrifice one's dearest desires in the cause of duty and right, than to snatch some brief joys out of life, and perish like the insects that are born and die in a day."

"I am so glad you can enjoy good poetry, dear,"

said Madoline, delighted at any surcease of frivolity
in her young sister.

"Enjoy it! I revel in it; it is my delight.
Pray don't suppose that I dislike books, Lina. Only
keep away from me grammars, and geographies, and
biographies of learned men, and voyages to the
North Pole—there is a South Pole, too, isn't there,
dear? though nobody even seems to worry about it
—and you may read me as many books as you like."

"How condescending of you, little one!" said
Madoline, smiling at the bright young face looking
up from the sofa-pillow, on which Daphne's golden
head reclined in luxurious restfulness. "Well,
I will read to you with pleasure. It will be my
delight to help to carry on your education; for
though girls learn an immense number of things
at school they don't seem to know much when
they come away. We will read together for a
couple of hours a day if you like, dear."

"Till Gerald comes home," retorted Daphne;
"he will not let you give me two hours of your
life every day. He will want you all to himself."

"He can join our studies; he is a great reader."

"Expose my ignorance to a future brother-in-law? Not for worlds!" cried Daphne. "Let us talk about him, Lina. Aren't you delighted to think he is coming home?"

"Yes; I am very glad."

"How do my father and Gerald get on together?"

"Not too well, I am sorry to say. Papa is fonder of Edgar than of Gerald. You know how prejudiced he is about race and high birth. I don't think he has ever quite forgiven Gerald his father's trade."

"But there is Lady Geraldine to fall back upon. Surely she makes amends."

"Hardly, according to papa's ideas. You see the Earldom of Heronville is only a creation of Charles the Second's reign, and his peerages are not always respectable. I believe there were scandals about the first countess. Her portrait by Sir Peter Lely hangs in the refectory at Goring Abbey. She was a very lovely woman, and Lady Geraldine was rather proud of being thought like her."

"Although she was not respectable," said Daphne. "And was there really a likeness?"

"Yes; and a marked one. I can see it even in Gerald, who is the image of his mother—the same dreamy eyes, the same thoughtful mouth. But you will be able to judge for yourself when Gerald comes home, for I have no doubt we shall be going over to the Abbey."

"The Abbey? It is a very old place, I suppose?"

"No; it was built by Mr. Goring."

"Why Abbey? Surely that means an old place that was once inhabited by monks."

"It was Mr. Goring's fancy. He insisted upon calling his house an abbey. It was foolish, of course; but, though he was a very good man, I believe he had a slight leaven of obstinacy in his disposition, and when once he made up his mind about anything he was not to be turned from his purpose."

"Perverse old creature! And is the Abbey nice?"

"It is as grand and as beautiful a place as

money could make it. There are cloisters copied
from those at Muckross, and the dining-room has
a Gothic roof, and is called a refectory. The
situation is positively lovely : a richly timbered
valley, sheltered by green hills."

"And you are to be mistress of this magnificent
place. Oh, Lina, what shall I do when you are
married, and I am left alone here *tête-à-tête* with
papa ? How shall I support my life ? "

"Dearest, by that time you will have learned
to understand your father, and you will be quite at
your ease with him."

"I think not. I am afraid he is one of those
mysteries which I shall never fathom."

" My love, that is such a foolish notion.
Besides, in a year or two my Daphne may have a
husband and a house of her own—perhaps a more
interesting place than Goring Abbey," added
Lina, thinking of Hawksyard, which seemed to
her Daphne's natural destination.

June ripened, and bloomed, and grew daily
more beautiful. It was peerless weather, with

just such blue skies and sunny noontides as there had been at Fontainebleau last year, but without the baking heat and the breathless atmosphere. Here there were cool winds to lift the rippling hair from Daphne's brow, and cool grass under her feet. She revelled in the summer beauty of the earth; she spent almost all her life out of doors, on the river, in the woods, in the garden. If she studied, it was under the spreading boughs of the low Spanish chestnut which made a tent of greenery on the lawn. Sometimes she carried her drawing-book to some point of vantage on a neighbouring hill, and sketched the outline of a wide range of landscape, and washed in a sky, and began a tree in the foreground, and left off in disgust. She never finished anything. Her portfolio was full of beginnings, not altogether devoid of talent: mouse-coloured cows, deep-red oxen, every kind of tree and rock and old English cottage, or rick-yard, or gray-stone village church; but nothing finished—the stamp of an impetuous, impatient temper upon all.

There had been no definite announcement as

to Gerald's return. He was in Sweden, seeing
wonderful falls and grottoes, which he described
in his letters to Madoline, and he was coming back
soon, perhaps before the end of July. He had
told the Abbey servants to be prepared for him
at any time. This indefiniteness kept Madoline's
mind in a somewhat perturbed state; yet she had
to be outwardly calm, and full of thoughtfulness
for her father, who required constant attention.
His love for his elder daughter was the one
redeeming grace of a selfish nature. It was a
selfish love, for he would have willingly let her
waste her life in maiden solitude for the sake of
keeping her by his side; but it was love, and this
was something in a man of so stern and unyielding
a temper.

He liked her to be always near him, always
within call, his companion abroad, his counsellor
at home. He consulted her about all the details
of his estate and her own, rarely wrote a business
letter without reading it to her. She was wanted
in his study continually. When he was tired after
a morning's business, she read the newspapers to

him, or a heavy political article in Blackwood or one of the Quarterlies, were he inclined to hear it. She never shirked a duty, or considered her own pleasure. She had educated herself to be her father's companion, and counted it a privilege to minister to him.

"Faultless daughter, perfect wife," said Sir Vernon, clasping her hand as she sat beside his sofa; "Goring is a lucky fellow to get such a prize."

"Why should he not have a good wife, dear father? He is good himself. Remember what a good son he was."

"To his mother, admirable. I doubt if he and old Goring hit it quite so well. I wish he came of a better stock."

"That is a prejudice of yours, father."

"It is a prejudice that I have rarely seen belied by experience. I wish you had chosen Edgar. There is a fine fellow for you, a lineal descendant of that Turchill who was sheriff of Warwickshire in the reign of the Confessor. Shakespeare's mother could trace her descent from the same stock. So you see that Edgar can claim alliance with the greatest poet of all time."

" I should never have thought it," said Madoline laughingly; "his lineage doesn't show itself in his conversation. I like him very much, you know, papa; indeed, I may say I love him, but it is in a thoroughly sisterly fashion. By-the-bye, papa, don't you think he might make an excellent husband for Daphne?" she faltered, with downcast eyes, as she went on with her crewel-work.

" She would be an uncommonly fortunate girl if she got him," retorted Sir Vernon, with a clouding countenance; " he is too good for her."

" Oh, father! can you speak like that of your own daughter ? " remonstrated Lina.

" Is a man to shut his eyes to a girl's character because she happens to bear his name ? " asked Sir Vernon impatiently. " Daphne is a lump of self-indulgent frivolity.

" Indeed you are mistaken," cried Lina; " she is very sweet-tempered and loving."

" Sweet-tempered! Yes; I know the kind of

thing. Winning words, pretty looks, trivial fascinations; a creature whose movements you watch
—fascinated by her variety—as you watch a
bird in a cage. Graceful, beautiful, false,
worthless! I have some experience of the
type."

"Father, this is the most cruel prejudice.
What can Daphne have ever done to offend
you ?"

"Done! Is she not her mother's daughter ?
Don't argue with me about her, Lina. She is
here beside my hearth, and I must make the
best of her. God grant she may come to no
harm; but I am full of fear when I think of her
future."

"Then you would be glad if Edgar were
to propose for her, and she were to accept
him ?"

"Certainly. It would be the very best thing
that could happen to her. I should only feel sorry
for him. But I don't think a man who once
loved you would ever content himself with
Daphne."

"He is very attentive to her."

"*Che sara, sara !*" murmured Sir Vernon,
languidly.

It was Midsummer-day—the hottest, brightest
day there had been yet, and Daphne had given
herself up to unmixed enjoyment of the warmth
and light and cloudless blue sky. Sir Vernon
and Madoline had a luncheon engagement at a
house beyond Stoneleigh, a drive of eleven miles
each way, so dinner had been postponed from
eight to half-past, and Daphne had the livelong
day to herself; free to follow her own devices,
free even from the company of her devoted slave
Edgar, who would have hung upon her like a
burr had he been at home, but who was spending
a few days in London with his mother, escorting
that somewhat homely matron to picture-galleries,
garden-parties, and theatres, and trying to rub
off a year's rural rust by a week's metropolitan
friction.

Edgar was away; the light park-phaeton with
the chestnuts had driven off at half-past eleven,

Madoline looking lovely in a Madras muslin gown and a bonnet made of roses, her father content to loll in the low seat by her side while she managed the somewhat vivacious cobs. Daphne watched the carriage till it vanished at a curve of the narrow wooded drive, and then ran back to the house to plan her own campaign.

" I will have a picnic," she said to herself, " a solitary, selfish, Robinson Crusoe-like picnic. I will have nobody but Tennyson and Lina's collie to keep me company. Goldie and I will go trespassing, and find a sly secret corner in Charlecote Park where we can eat our luncheon. I believe it is against the law to stray from the miserable footpath; but who cares for law on Midsummer-day? I shall feel myself almost as brave as Shakespeare when he went poaching; and, thank goodness, there is no Justice Shallow to call me to order."

She ran to her own room for a basket, a picturesque beehive basket, the very one she had carried — and he had carried — at Fontainebleau. What a foolish impulse it must have been which made her touch the senseless straw with her lips, remembering whose hand had held it! Then to the housekeeper's room to forage for provisions. The wing of a chicken; a thick wedge of pound-cake; a punnet of strawberries; a bottle of lemonade; a couple of milk-rolls. Mrs. Spicer would have packed these things neatly in white paper, but Daphne bundled them into the basket anyhow.

"Don't trouble, you dear good soul; they are only for Goldie and me," she said.

"You may just as well have things nice, miss. There, you'd have forgot the salt if I wasn't here. And if you're going to take that there obstreperous collie you'll want something more substantial."

"Give me a slice of beef for him then, and a couple more of your delicious rolls," asked Daphne coaxingly. "My Goldie mustn't be starved. And be quick, like a love, for I'm in an awful hurry."

"Lor, miss, when you've got all the day before you! You'll be fearful lonesome."

"What, with Goldie and the 'Idylls of the King!'" exclaimed Daphne, glancing downwards at her little green cloth volume.

"Ah, well; I know when young ladies have got a nice novel to read they never feel lonesome," said Mrs. Spicer, filling every available corner of the basket, with which Daphne stepped off gaily to summon Goldie.

Goldie was a bright yellow collie, intensely vivacious, sharp-nosed, brown-eyed; a dog that knew not what it was to be quiet; a dog you might lose at the other end of the county, confident that he would scamper home across wood and hill and valley as straight as the crow's flight. He spent half his life tied up in the stable-yard, and the other half rushing about the country with Daphne. He travelled an incalculable number of miles in the course of an ordinary walk, and was given to racing cattle. He worshipped Daphne, and held her in some awe on this cattle question; would leap into the air with mad delight when she was kind to him, or grovel at her feet whe she was angry.

"Now, Goldie dear, if you and I are to lunch in Charlecote Park, I must take a strap for you," said Daphne, as they started from the stable-yard, Goldie proclaiming his rapture by clamorous barking. "It will never do for you to go racing the Lucy deer, or even the Lucy oxen. We should get into worse trouble than Shakespeare did, for Shakespeare had not such a frigid father as mine. I daresay old John, the glover, was an easy-going indulgent soul whom his son could treat anyhow."

It was only a walk of two miles across the fields to Charlecote; two miles by meadows that are as lovely and as richly timbered as they could have been in Shakespeare's time. High farming is not yet the rule in Warwickshire. Hedges grow high and wild; broad oaks spread their kingly branches above the rich rank grass; dock and mallow, foxglove, fern, and dog-rose thrive and bloom beside every ditch; and many a fair stretch of grass by the roadside—a no man's land of plea-sant pasture—offers space for the hawker's van, or the children's noonday sports, or the repose of the

tired tramp, lying face downwards in a rapture of
rest, while the skylark trills in the distant blue
above him, and the rustle of summer leaves soothes
his slumber.

It is a lovely country, lovely in its simple,
pastoral, English beauty, calm and fitting cradle for
a great mind.

After the fields came a lane, a green arcade with
a leafy roof, through which the sun-rays crept in
quivering lines of light, and then the gate that
opened on the footpath across Charlecote Park.
Yonder showed the gray walls of the house, venerable on one side, modern on the other, and the stone
single-arched bridge, and the lake, narrowing to a
dull sluggish-looking stream that seemed to flow
nowhere in particular. The tallest and stoutest of
the elms looked too young for Shakespeare's time.
But here and there appeared the ruin of a
tree, hollow of trunk, gaunt of limb, whose green
branches may once have sheltered the deer he stole.

The place was very lonely. There was nobody
to interfere with Daphne's pleasure, or even to
object to the collie, who crept meekly to her side,

held by a strap, and casting longing looks at the
distant oxen. She wandered about in the loneliest
bits of the park, supremely indifferent to rules and
regulations as to where she might go and where
she might not; till she finally deposited her basket
and sunshade under a stalwart oak, and sat down
at the foot thereof, with Goldie still strapped, and
constrained to virtue. She fastened one end of the
strap to the lowest branch of the tree, Goldie standing on end licking her hands all the time.

"Now, dear, you are as comfortable as in your
own stable-yard. You can admire the cows and
sheep in the distance, standing about so peacefully
in the sunshine, as if they had never heard of sunstroke, but you can't hunt them. And now you
shall have your dinner."

It was a very quiet picnic, perhaps even a
trifle dull; though, at the worst, it might be better
to picnic alone among the four-footed beasts in
Charlecote Park, than to assume a forced gaiety
in a party of stupid people, at the conventional,
banquet of doubtful lobster and tepid champagne,
in one of the time-honoured haunts of the cockney

picnicker. Daphne thought of Midsummer-day
in the year that was gone, as she sat eating her
chicken and sipping her lemonade, half of which
had been lost in the process of uncorking. How
gay she had been, how foolishly, unreasonably
glad! And now a great deal of the flavour had
gone out of life since her seventeenth birthday.

"How happy Lina looks, now that the time
for her lover's return draws near!" she thought.
"She has something to look forward to, some
reason for counting the days; while to me time
is all alike, one week just the same as another.
I am a horribly selfish creature. I ought to
feel glad of her gladness; I ought to rejoice in
her joy. But Nature made me out of poor stuff,
didn't she, Goldie dear?"

She laid her bright head on the collie's tawny
coat. The pale gold of her soft flowing hair contrasted and yet harmonised with the ruddy hue
of the dog, and made a picture fair to look upon.
But there was no one wandering in Charlecote
Park to paint Daphne's portrait. She was very
lucky in not being discovered by a party of eager

Americans, spectacled, waterproofed, hyper-intelligent, and knowing a great deal more about Shakespeare's biography than is known to the duller remnant of the Anglo-Saxon race still extant on this side the Atlantic.

She ate her strawberries in dreamy thoughtfulness, and fed Goldie to repletion, till he stretched himself luxuriously upon her gown, and dreamed of a chase he was too lazy to follow, had he been ever so free. Then she shut the empty basket, propped herself up against the rugged old trunk, and opened the "Idylls." It is a book to be read over and over again, for ever and ever, just one of those rare books of which the soul knows no weariness—like Shakespeare, or Goethe's Faust, or Childe Harold—a book to be opened, haphazard, anywhere.

But Daphne did not so open the volume. Elaine was her poem of poems, and it was Elaine she read to-day in that placid shade amidst green pastures and venerable trees, under a cloudless sky. Launcelot was her ideal man—faulty, but more lovable in his faultiness than even the perfect

Arthur. Yet what woman would not wish—aye, even the guilty one grovelling at his feet—to be Arthur's wife ?

She read slowly, pondering every word, for that fair young Saxon was to her a very real personage—a being whose sorrows gave her absolute pain as she read. Time had been when she could not read Elaine's story without tears, but to-day her eyes were dry, even to the last, when her fancy saw the barge gliding silently down the stream, with the fair dead face looking up to the sky, and the waxen hands meekly folded above the heart that had broken for love of Launcelot.

"I wonder how long his sorrow lasted," she thought, as she closed the book ; and then she clasped her hands above the fair head resting against the rugged bark of the oak, and gave herself up to day-dreams, and let the afternoon wear on as it might, in placid enjoyment of the atmosphere and the landscape.

Charlecote church clock had struck five when she plucked herself out of dreamland with an effort, unstrapped her dog from the tree, took up her empty basket, and started on the journey **home**. She had ample leisure for her walk. Dinner was not to be until half-past eight, and Sir Vernon and **his** daughter were hardly likely to be **back** till dinner-time.

It **was a stately feast to which they** had been bidden—a feast in honour of somebody's coming of age : **a champagne breakfast for the quality,** roasted **oxen and** strong ale for the commonalty, speechifying, military bands — an altogether ponderous entertainment. Sir Vernon had groaned over the inevitable weariness of the affair in advance, and **had** talked of himself as a martyr to neighbourly feeling.

The homeward walk in the quiet afternoon light was delicious. Goldie, released from his strap **directly** they left Charlecote, ran and leapt like **a creature** possessed. Oh, how he enjoyed himself with the first herd they came to, scampering after **innocent** milch-cows, and endangering his life by flying at the foreheads of horned oxen ! Daphne let him do as he **liked**. She wandered out of her way a little to follow the windings of her beloved river. It was between seven and eight when she despatched Goldie to his stable-yard, and went into the cool shady hall, where two old orange-trees in great green crockery tubs scented the air.

The butler met her on her way to the morning-room.

"Oh, if you please, Miss Daphne, Mr. Goring has arrived, and would like to see you before you dress for dinner. He was so disappointed at finding Miss Lawford away from home, and he would like to have a talk with you."

Daphne looked at the tumbled white gown— it was the same she had worn last year at Fontainebleau—and thought of her towzled hair. "I am so shamefully untidy," she said; "I think I had better dress first, Brooks."

"Oh, don't, Miss Daphne. You look nice enough, I'm sure. And I daresay Mr. Goring is impatient to hear all about Miss Lawford, or he wouldn't have asked so particular to see you."

"Of course not. No; perhaps he won't notice my untidiness. I'll risk it. Yet first impressions—— I don't want him to think me an underbred school-girl," muttered Daphne as she opened the drawing-room door.

The room was large, and full of flowers and objects that broke the view; and all the glow and glory of a summer sunset was shining in at the wide west window.

For a moment or so Daphne could see no one; the room seemed empty of humanity. There was the American squirrel revolving in his big airy cage; there lay Fluff, the Maltese terrier, curled into a silky ball in a corner of the sofa; and that seemed all. But as Daphne went timidly towards the window, a figure rose from a low chair, a face turned to meet her.

She lifted her clasped hands to her breast with a startled cry.

"Nero!"

"Poppæa!"

CHAPTER IX.

"OF COLOUR PALE AND DEAD WAS SHE."

"AND so you are Daphne?" said Mr. Goring, taking both her hands, and looking at her with an amused smile, not without tender admiration of the fair pale face and widely-opened blue eyes. Months afterwards he remembered the scared look in those lovely eyes, the death-like pallor of the complexion; but just now he ascribed Daphne's evident agitation to a school-girl's natural discomfiture at being found out in a risky escapade.

"And so you are Daphne?" he repeated. "Why, you told me your father was a grocer in Oxford Street. Was not that what school-boys call a crumper?"

"No," said Daphne, recovering herself, and a sparkle of mischief lighting up her eyes; "it was strictly true—of Martha Dibb's father."

"And you adopted your friend's parent for the nonce; a thoroughly Roman custom that of adoption, and in harmony with your Roman name. By the way, were you christened Poppæa Daphne, or Daphne Poppæa?"

He had been amusing himself with the squirrel for the last half-hour; but he found Daphne's embarrassment ever so much more amusing than the squirrel. He felt no more seriously about the one than about the other.

"Don't," exclaimed Daphne; "you must have known quite well from the first moment that my name wasn't Poppæa, just as well as I knew that yours wasn't Nero."

"Well, I had a shrewd suspicion that you were romancing about the name; but I swallowed the grocer. That was too bad of you. Do you know that you made me quite unhappy? I was miserable at the idea that such a girl as you could be allied with grocery. A ridiculous prejudice, was it not, in a man whose father began life as a day-labourer ? ''

Daphne had sunk into a low chair by the squirrel's cage, and was feeding that pampered favourite with the green points of some choice conifer. She seemed more taken up by his movements than by her future brother-in-law. Her agitation had passed, yet she was pale still, only the faintest bloom in her fair cheek, the pink of a wild-rose.

" Please don't tell Lina," she pleaded, with her eyes on the squirrel.

" Oh, she doesn't know anything about it then ?"

"Not a word. I dared not tell her. When I tried to do so, I became suddenly aware how horridly I had behaved. Martha Dibb and I were silly, thoughtless creatures, acting on the impulse of the moment."

" I don't think there was much impulse about Miss Dibb," said Mr. Goring " t seemed to me that she only looked on.

" It is disgustingly mean of you to say that ! " exclaimed Daphne, recurring to her school-girl

phraseology, which she had somewhat modified
at South Hill.

"Forgive me. And I must really hold my
tongue about our delicious picnics? Of course
I shall obey you, little one. But I hate secrets,
and am a bad hand at keeping them. I shall
never forget those two happy days at Fontainebleau. How strange that you and I, who were
destined to become brother and sister, should
make each other's acquaintance in that haphazard,
informal fashion! It seemed almost as if we were
fated to meet, didn't it?"

"Was that the fate you read in my hand?"

"No," he answered, suddenly grave; "that
was not what I read. Pshaw," he added in a lighter
tone, "chiromancy is all nonsense. Why should
a man, not too much given to belief in the things
that are good for him to believe, pin his faith on
a fanciful science of that kind? I have left off
looking at palms ever since that day at Fontainebleau. And now tell me about your sister. I am
longing to see her. To think that I should have
stumbled on just the one particular afternoon on

which she was to be so long away! I pictured her sitting by yonder bamboo table, like Penelope waiting for her Odysseus. Do you know that I have come straight through from Bergen without stopping?"

"And you have not been home to your Abbey?"

"My Abbey will keep. By-the-bye, how is the place looking—the gardens all in their beauty, I suppose?"

"I have never seen it."

"Never! Why, I thought Lina would be driving over once or twice a week to survey her future domain. I take it positively unkind that you have never seen my Abbey: my cloisters where never monk walked; my refectory, where never monk ate; my chapel, where no priest ever said mass. I should have thought curiosity would have impelled you to go and look at Goring Abbey. It is such a charming anomaly. But it pleased my poor father to build it, so I must not complain."

"I think you ought to be very proud of it when you consider how hard your father must

have worked for the money it cost," said Daphne
bluntly.

"Yes, John Giles had to put a long career
of honest labour behind him, before he became
Giles Goring and owner of Goring Abbey. He
was a good old man. I feel sorry sometimes that
I am not more like him."

"Lina says you are like your mother."

"Yes, I believe I resemble her side of the house.
It was by no means the more meritorious side,
for the Heronvilles were always loose fish, while
my father was one of the best men who ever wore
shoe-leather. Do you think Lina will be pleasantly
surprised by my return?"

"Do I think it?" echoed Daphne. "Why,
she has been longing for your coming—counting
every hour. I know that, though she has not
said as much. I can read her thoughts."

"Clever little puss. Daphne, do you know
I am quite delighted to find that my grocer's
daughter of Fontainebleau Forest is to be my
new sister."

"You are very good," returned Daphne rather

stiffly. "It is eight o'clock, so I think, if you'll excuse me, I had better go and dress for dinner."

"Wait till your people come home. I've ever so many questions to ask."

"There is the carriage! You can ask them of Lina herself."

She ran out of the room by the glass door leading into the conservatory, leaving Mr. Goring to meet his betrothed at the opposite door. She ran through the conservatory to the garden. The sun was sinking in a sea of many-coloured clouds, yonder on the edge of the hills, and the river at the bottom of the valley ran between the rushes like liquid gold. Daphne stood on the sloping lawn staring at the light like a bewildered creature.

She stood thus for some minutes motionless, with clasped hands, gazing at the sunset. Then she turned and walked slowly back to the house. There was no one to watch her, no one to think of her at this moment. Gerald and Lina were together in the drawing-room, steeped in the rapture of reunion.

"Let me be rational, let me be reasonable, if I can," Daphne said to herself. She re-entered the house by an obscure door at the east end, and went up to her own room. There, in the soft evening light, she cast herself upon her knees by the bed, and prayed : prayed with all the fervour of her untried soul, prayed that she might be kept from temptation and led to do the thing that was right. Prayer so earnest in a nature so light and reckless was a new experience. She rose from her knees like a new creature, and fancied she had plucked the evil weed of a fatal fancy out of her heart. She moved about her room calmly and quietly, dressed herself carefully, and went back to the drawing-room, two minutes before the half-hour, radiant and smiling.

Madoline was still in the gown she had worn at the *déjeûner*. She had taken off her hat, and that was all, too happy in her lover's company to spare five minutes for the revision of her toilet. Gerald had done nothing to improve his travelling attire. Even the dust of the long railroad journey from Hull was still upon his clothes.

"Gerald tells me that you and he have made friends already, Daphne," said Lina in a happy voice.

She was standing by her lover's side in front of the open window, while Sir Vernon sat in an easy-chair devouring his *Times*, and trying to make up for the lost hours since the post came in.

"Yes; Daphne and I have sworn eternal friendship," exclaimed Gerald gaily. "We mean to be a most devoted brother and sister. It was quite wonderful how quickly we broke the ice, and how thoroughly at home we became in a quarter of an hour."

"Daphne is not a very terrible personage," said Madoline, smiling at her sister's bright young face. "Well, darling, had you a happy day all by yourself? I was almost glad you were not with us. The coming of age was a very tiresome business. I had ten times rather have been in our own gardens with you."

"The whole entertainment was ineffably dull," said Sir Vernon, without looking from his paper.

And now the well-bred butler glided across

the threshold, and gently insinuated that dinner
was served, if it might be the pleasure of his people
to come and eat it: whereupon Mr. Goring gave
his arm to Madoline, and Sir Vernon for the first
time since his younger daughter's return felt
himself constrained to escort her to the dining-
room, or leave her to follow in his wake like a
lap-dog.

He deliberated for a moment or two as to which
he should do, then made a hook of his elbow, and
looked down at her dubiously, as much as to say
that she might take it or leave it.

Daphne would have much liked to refuse the
proffered boon, but she was in a dutiful mood
to-night, so she meekly slipped her little gloved
hand under her parent's sleeve, and walked by
his side to the dining-room, where he let her hand
drop directly they were inside the door.

Everyone at South Hill hated a glare, so the
dining-room, like the drawing-room, was lighted
by moderator lamps under velvet shades. Two
large brazen lamps with deep-fringed purple
shades hung a little way above the table; two

more lighted the sideboard. The French windows stood wide open, and across a balcony full of flowers appeared the shadowy landscape and the cool evening sky.

Sir Vernon was tired and out of spirits. He had very little to say about anything except the proceedings of the afternoon, and all his remarks upon the hospitalities at which he had assisted were of an abusive character. He could eat no dinner, his internal economy having been thrown altogether out of gear by the barbarity of a solid meal at three o'clock. His discontent would have effectually damped the spirits of any human beings except lovers. Those privileged beings inhabit a world of their own; so Madoline and Gerald smiled at each other, and talked to each other across the roses and lilies that beautified the dinner-table, and seemed unconscious that anything unpleasant was going on.

Daphne watched them thoughtfully. How lovely her sister looked in the new light of this perfect happiness—how unaffectedly she revealed her delight at her lover's return!

" How good it was of you to come back a month sooner than you had promised, Gerald!" she said.

"My dear girl, I have been pining to come home for the last six months, but, as you and your father and I had chalked out a certain portion of Europe which I was to travel over, I thought I ought to go through with it; but if you knew how heartily sick I am of going from pillar to post, of craning my neck to look at the roofs of churches, and dancing attendance upon grubby old sacristans, and riding up narrow pathways on mules, and having myself and my luggage registered through from the bustling commercial city I am sick of to loathing after twenty-four hours' experience, to the sleepy mediæval town which I inevitably tire of in ten, you would be able to understand my delight in coming back to you and placid Warwick-shire. By-the-bye, why didn't you take Daphne to see the Abbey? She tells me she has never been over to Goring."

" I should have had no pleasure in showing her your house "—" Our house," interjected Gerald— " while you were away."

"Well, dearest, it was a loving fancy, so I won't scold you for it. We'll have a——" He paused for an instant, looking at Daphne with a mischievous smile. "We'll have a picnic there to-morrow."

"Why a picnic?" grumbled Sir Vernon. "I can understand people eating out of doors when they have no house to shelter them, but nobody but an idiot would squat on the grass to dine if he could get at chairs and tables. Look at your gipsies and hawkers now—you seldom catch them picnicking. If their tent or their caravan is ever so small and stuffy they generally feed inside it."

"Never mind the hawkers," exclaimed Gerald contemptuously. "A fig for common-sense. Of course, everybody in his senses knows that such a dinner as this is much more comfortable than the most perfect picnic that ever was organised. But, for all that, I adore picnics; and we'll have one to-morrow, won't we, Daphne?"

He looked across the table at her in the subdued lamp-light, smiling, and expecting to see a responsive smile in her eyes : but she was preternaturally grave.

"Just as you like," she said.

"Just as I like! What a chilling repulse! Why, unless Madoline and you approve of the idea, I don't care a straw for it. I'll punish you for your indifference, Miss Daphne. You shall have a formal luncheon in the refectory, at a table large enough for thirty, and groaning under my father's family plate—Garrard's, of the reign of Victoria, strictly ponderous and utilitarian. What a lovely light there is in the western sky!" said Gerald, as Madoline and her sister rose from the table. "Shall we all walk down to the river, before we join Sir Vernon in the billiard-room ? You'd like to try your hand against me, sir, I suppose, now that I come fresh from benighted lands where the tables have no pockets."

"Yes; I'll play a game with you presently."

Gerald and the two girls went into the verandah, and thence by a flight of shallow steps to the lawn. It was a peerless night after a peerless day. A young moon was shining above the topmost branches of the deodaras, and touching the Avon with patches of silvery light. The scene was lovely, the atmosphere delicious, but Daphne felt that she was one too many, though Madoline had linked an arm through hers. Those two had so much to talk about, so many questions to ask each other.

"And you have really come home for good," said Madoline.

"For good, dearest; for the brightest fate that can befall a man, to marry the woman he loves and settle down to a peaceful placid life in the home of his—ancestor. I have been a rover quite long enough, and I shall rove no more, except at your command."

"There are places I should love to visit with you, Gerald—Switzerland, Italy, the Tyrol."

"We will go wherever you please, dearest. It will be delightful to me to show you all that is fairest on this earth, and to hear you say, when we are hunting vainly for some undiscovered nook,

where we may escape from the tourist herd—
'After all, there is no place like home.' "

" I shall only be too much inclined to say that.
I love our own country, and the scenery I have
known all my life."

" We must start early to-morrow, Lina. We
have a great deal of business to get through at
the Abbey."

" Business ! "

" Yes, dear; I want you to give me your ideas
about the building of new hot-houses. With your
passion for flowers the present amount of glass will
never be enough. What do you say to sending
MacCloskie over to meet us there ? His opinion
as a practical man might be of use."

" If Mr. MacCloskie is going to picnic with
you I'll stay at home," said Daphne. " I admire
the gentleman as a gardener, but I detest him as
a human being."

" Don't be frightened, Daphne," said Gerald,
laughing. " It is a levelling age, but we have not
yet come to picnicking with our gardeners."

"Mr. MacCloskie is such a very superior person," retorted Daphne, "I don't know what he might expect."

They had strolled down to the meadow by the river, a long stretch of level pasture, richly timbered, divided from the gardens by a ha-ha, over which there was a light iron bridge. They lingered for a little while by this bridge, looking across at the river.

"Do you know that Daphne has started a boat," said Madoline, "and has become very expert with a pair of sculls? She rowed me down to Stratford the day before yesterday, and back against the stream."

"Indeed! I congratulate you on a delightful accomplishment, Daphne. I don't see why girls should not have their pleasure out of the river as well as boys. I've a brilliant idea. The Abbey is only five miles up the stream. Suppose we charter Daphne's boat for to-morrow. I can pull a pretty good stroke, and the distance will be easy between us two. Will your boat hold three of us comfortably, do you think, Daphne?"

"It would hold six."

"Then consider your services retained for to-morrow. I shall enjoy the miniature prettiness of the Avon, after the mightier streams I have been upon lately."

"I don't suppose Lina would like it," faltered Daphne, not appearing elated at the idea.

"Lina would like it immensely," said her sister. "I shall feel so safe if you are with us, Gerald. What a strange girl you are, Daphne! A week ago you were eager to carry me to the end of the world in your boat."

"You can have the boat, of course, if you like, and I'll pull, if you want me," returned Daphne, somewhat ungraciously; "but I think you'll find five miles of the Avon rather a monotonous busi-ness. It is a very lovely river if you take it in sections, but as both banks present a succession of green fields and pollard willows, it is just possible for the human mind to tire of it."

"Daphne, you are an absolute cynic—and at seventeen!" exclaimed Gerald, with pretended horror. "What will you be by the time you are forty?"

"If I am alive I daresay I shall be a very horrid old woman," said Daphne. "Perhaps something after the pattern of Aunt Rhoda. I can't conceive anything much worse than that."

"Papa will be waiting for his game of billiards," said Lina. "We had better hurry back to th house."

They were met on the threshold of the conservatory by Mrs. Ferrers. That lady had a wonderful knack of getting acquainted with everything that happened at South Hill. If there had been a semaphore on the roof she could hardly have known things sooner.

"My dear Gerald, what a delightful surprise you have given us!" she exclaimed. "I put on my hat the instant the Rector had said grace. I left him to drink his claret alone—a thing that has not happened since we were married—and walked over to bid you welcome. How well you are looking! How very brown you have grown! I am so glad to see you."

"It was very good of you to come over on purpose, Mrs. Ferrers."

"May I not be Aunt Rhoda instead of Mrs. Ferrers? I should like it ever so much better. Next year I shall be really your aunt, you know."

"And the Rector will be your uncle," said Daphne pertly. "He is mine already, and he is ever so much kinder than when I was only his parishioner."

Mrs. Ferrers shot a piercing look, half angry, half interrogative, at her younger niece. The Rector had shown a reprehensible tendency to praise the girl's beauty, had on one occasion gone so far as to offer her a patriarchal kiss, from which Daphne had recoiled involuntarily, saying afterwards to her sister that "one must draw the line somewhere."

"Vernon has gone to bed," said Aunt Rhoda; "he felt thoroughly wearied out after the gathering at Holmsley, which seems from his account to have been a very dull business. I am glad the Rector and I declined. A cold luncheon is positive death to him."

"Then we needn't go indoors yet awhile," said

Gerald. "It is lovely out here. Shall I fetch a wrap for you, Lina?"

Mrs. Ferrers was carefully draped in her China-crape shawl, one of Madoline's wedding gifts to her aunt, and costly enough for a royal present.

"Thanks. There is a shawl on a sofa in the drawing-room."

"Let Daphne fetch it," interjected Mrs. Ferrers; and her niece flew to obey, while the other three sauntered slowly along the broad terrace in front of the windows.

There were some light iron chairs and a table at one end of the walk, and here they seated themselves to enjoy the summer night.

"As our English summer is a matter of about five weeks, broken by a good deal of storm and rain, we ought to make the most of it," remarked Gerald. "I hope we shall have a fine day for the Abbey to-morrow."

"You are going to take Lina to the Abbey?"

"Yes, for a regular businesslike inspection; that we may see what will have to be improved

or altered, or added, or done away with before
next year."

"How interesting! I should like so much
to drive over with you. My experience in
housekeeping matters might possibly be of use."

"Invaluable, no doubt," answered Gerald, with
his easy-going, half listless air; "but we must
postpone that advantage until the next time. We
are going in Daphne's boat, which will only comfortably hold three," said Gerald, with a calm
contempt for actual truth which horrified Madoline,
who was rigidly truthful even in the most trivial
things.

"Going in Daphne's boat! What an absurd
idea !"

"Don't say that, Aunt Rhoda, for it's my
idea," remonstrated Gerald.

"But I can't help saying it. When you have
half-a-dozen carriages at your disposal, and
when the drive to Goring is absolutely lovely,
to go in a horrid little boat."

"It is a very nice boat, Aunt Rhoda, and
Daphne manages it capitally," said Lina.

"I think it will be a delightfully dreamy way of going," said Gerald. "We shall take our time about it. There is no reason we should hurry. I shall order a carriage to meet us at the bottom of Goring Lane, where we shall land. If we prefer to drive home we can do so."

"My dear Gerald, you and Madoline are the best judges of what is agreeable to yourselves; but I cannot help thinking that you are encouraging Daphne in a most unbecoming pursuit."

The appearance of Daphne herself with the shawl put a stop to the argument. She folded the soft woollen wrap round her sister, and then stooped to kiss her.

"Good-night, Lina," she said.

"Going to bed so early, Daphne? I hope you are not ill."

"Only a little tired after my rambles. Good-night, Aunt Rhoda; good-night, Mr. Goring," and Daphne ran away.

"Aunt Rhoda might drive over and meet us at Goring, Gerald," suggested Madoline, who was always thoughtful of other people's pleasure

and did not wish her aunt to fancy herself
ignored.

"Certainly. I shall be charmed, if you think
it worth your while," said Gerald.

"Then I shall certainly come. My ponies
want exercise, and to-morrow is one of the Rector's
parochial days, so he won't miss me for an hour
or two. What time do you contemplate arriving
at the Abbey?"

"Oh, I suppose between one and two, the
orthodox luncheon-hour," answered Gerald.

Daphne was up and dressed before five o'clock
next morning. She had set her little American
alarum-clock for five; but that had been a needless
precaution, since she had not slept above a quarter
of an hour at a time all through the short summer
night. She had seen the last glimmer of the
fading moon, the first faint glow of sunlight
flickering on her wall. She stole softly downstairs,
unlocked doors and drew bolts with the silent
dexterity of a professional housebreaker, feeling
almost as guilty as if she had been one; and in
the cool quiet morning, while all the world beside

herself seemed asleep, she ran lightly across the
dewy lawn, down to the iron bridge by which she
had stood with Madoline and Gerald last night.
Then she crossed the meadow, wading ankle-deep
in wet grass, and scaring the placid kine, and
thus to the boat-house.

She went in and got into her boat, which
was drawn up under cover, and carefully protected
by linen clothing. She whisked the covering off,
and seated herself on the floor of the boat in
front of the place of honour, above which appeared
the name of the craft, in gilded letters on the
polished pine—" Nero."

She took out her penknife and began carefully,
laboriously, to scrape away the gilt lettering.
The thing had been so conscientiously done, the
letters were so sunk and branded into the wood,
that the task seemed endless; she was still digging
and scraping at the first letter when Arden church
clock struck six, every stroke floating clear and
sweet across the river.

" What—an—utter—idiot I was ! " she said to
herself, in an exasperated tone, emphasizing each

word with a savage dig of her knife into the gilded wood. "And how shall I ever get all these letters out before breakfast time?"

"Why attempt it?" asked a low pleasant voice close at hand, and Daphne, becoming suddenly aware of the odour of tobacco mixed with the perfumes of a summer meadow, looked up and saw Gerald Goring lounging against the door-post, smoking a cigarette.

"Why erase the name?" he asked. "It is a very good name—classical, historical, and not altogether inappropriate. Nero was a boat-builder himself, you know."

"Was he?" said Daphne, sitting limply in the bottom of her boat, completely unnerved.

"Yes; the vessel he built was a failure, or at any rate the result of his experiment was unsatisfactory, but the intention was original, and deserves praise. I am sorry you have spoilt the first letter of his name."

"Don't distress yourself," exclaimed Daphne, jumping up and stepping briskly out of her boat. "I am going to change the name of my boat, and

I thought I could do it this morning as a surprise for Lina; but it was a more difficult business than I supposed. And now I must run home as fast as I can, and make myself tidy for breakfast. My father is the essence of punctuality."

"But as half-past eight is his breakfast hour you need not be in a desperate hurry. It has only just struck six. Will you come for a stroll ?"

"No, thank you. I have ever so much to do before breakfast."

"Czerny's 'Studies of Velocity' ?"

"No."

"French grammar ?"

"No."

"Be sure you are ready to start directly after breakfast."

Daphne scampered off through the wet grass, leaving Mr. Goring standing by the boat-house door, looking down with an amused smile at the mutilated name.

CHAPTER X.

AT ten o'clock Daphne was down at the boat-house
again, ready for the aquatic excursion, looking as
fresh and bright as if nothing had ever occurred
to vex her. She wore a workmanlike attire of
indigo serge—no gay fluttering scarlet ribbons this
time. Her whole costume was studiously plain,
from the sailor hat to the stout Cromwell shoe
and dark blue stocking, the wash-leather glove
and leathern belt with a broad steel buckle.
Madoline's flowing muslin skirts and flowery hat
contrasted charmingly with her sister's more
masculine attire.

"This looks like business," said Gerald, as

Bink ran the boat into the water, and held her while the ladies stepped on board. "Now, Daphne, whichever of us gets tired first must forfeit a dozen pairs of gloves."

"I think it will be you, from the look of you," returned Daphne, as she rolled up her sleeves and took hold of an oar in an off-hand waterman-like manner. "When you are tired I'll take the sculls."

"Well, you see I am likely to be in very bad form. It is four years since I rowed in the 'Varsity race."

"What, you rowed in the great race? What affectation to talk about being in bad form. I should think a man could never forget training of that kind."

"He can never forget the theory, but he may feel the want of practice. However, I fancy I shall survive till we get to Goring Lane, and that you'll win no gloves to-day. I suppose you never wear anything less than twelve buttons?"

"Madoline gives me plenty of gloves, thank you," replied Daphne with dignity. "My glove-box is not supported by voluntary contributions."

"Daphne, do you know that for a young woman who is speedily to become my sister, you are barely civil?" said Gerald.

"I beg your pardon, I am practising a sisterly manner. I never met with a brother and sister yet who were particularly civil to each other."

They were rowing quietly up the stream, lowering their heads now and then to clear the drooping tresses of a willow. The verdant banks, the perpetual willows, were beautiful, but with a monotonous beauty. It was the ripe middle of the year, when all things are of one rich green—meadows and woods and hills—and in a country chiefly pastoral there must needs be a touch of sameness in the landscape. Here and there a spire showed above the trees, or a gray stone mansion stood boldly out upon the green hillside.

Daphne had so arranged cushions and wraps upon the principal seat as to conceal the mutilated name. Gerald rowed stroke, she sat in the bows, and Madoline reclined luxuriously in the stern with the Maltese terrier Fluff in her lap.

"If we are lucky we shall be at the Abbey

an hour and a half before your aunt and her ponies," said Gerald. "It was extremely obliging of her to volunteer the inestimable boon of her advice, but I fancy we should get on quite as well without her."

"It would have been unkind to let her think we didn't want her," said Madoline deprecatingly.

"That is so like you, Lina; you will go through life putting up with people you don't care about, rather than wound their feelings," said Gerald carelessly.

"Aunt Rhoda is my father's only sister. I am bound to respect her."

"I've no doubt the Old Man of the Sea was a very estimable person in the abstract," said Gerald, "but Sindbad shunted him at the first opportunity. Don't look so distressed, dearest. Aunt Rhoda shall patronise us, and dictate to us all our lives, if it please you. By-the-bye, what has become of your devoted slave and ally, Turchill? I expected to find him on the premises when I arrived at South Hill."

"He went up to London last week with his

mother, to make a round of the theatres and picture-galleries. **They will** be home in a **few** days, I daresay."

"I wonder he can exist out of Warwickshire. **He is so** thoroughly bucolic, **so** permeated by the **flavour of his** native soil."

"He is very kind and **good and** true-hearted," protested Daphne, **flushing indignantly** ; "and he is your old friend **and** kinsman. I wonder you can speak **so contemptuously** of **him,** Mr. Goring."

"What, my vixenish little Pop—Daphne," cried Gerald, colouring at this **slip** of the tongue, "is **it** thus the cat jumps ? I would not underrate Edgar for **worlds.** He is out and away the best fellow **I** know ; but, however much **you** may admire him, little one, that his mind is essentially **bucolic is a** fact—and facts are stubborn things."

"**You** have no right **to say** that I admire him. I respect and esteem him, and I am not ashamed to own **as much,** though you may think it a reason for laughing at me," retorted Daphne, still **angry.** "He taught me **to** row this very boat. He used to get up every morning at a ridiculously early hour, in order to be at South Hill in time to give me a lesson before breakfast."

"A man might do twice as much for your *beaux yeux*, and yet deem it no self-sacrifice."

"Don't," cried Daphne. "Didn't I tell you ages ago that I detest you when you flatter me."

Madoline looked up with momentary wonder at that expression "ages ago;" but Daphne was so given to wild exaggerations and a school-girl latitude of phrase, that "ages ago" might naturally mean yesterday.

"Daphne dearest, what has put you out of temper?" she asked gently. "I'm afraid you're getting tired."

"If she give in before we get to Goring Lane I shall claim a dozen pairs of gloves."

"I am not the least little bit tired; I could row you to Naseby, if you liked," replied Daphne haughtily; whereupon the lovers began to talk of their own affairs, somewhat lazily, as suited the summer morning and the quiet landscape, where a light haze that yet lingered over the fields seemed the cool and misty forecast of a blazing afternoon.

Goring Lane was an accommodation road, leading down from the home farm to the meadows on the river bank, and here they found a light open carriage and a pair of strong country-made gray horses waiting for them.

Gerald had sent his valet over before breakfast to make all arrangements for their reception. The man was waiting beside the carriage, and to Daphne's horror she beheld in him the grave gentleman in gray who had helped to convey provisions for the Fontainebleau picnic : but not a muscle of the valet's face betrayed the fact that he had ever seen this young lady before.

At the end of the lane they came into a shady park-like avenue, and then to a gray stone gateway, pillared, mediæval, grandiose; on the summit of each granite pillar a griffin of the most correct heraldic make grasped a shield, and on the shield were quarterings that hinted at a palmer's pilgrimage in the Holy Land, and a ragged staff that suggested kindred with the historic race of Dudley.

The lodge-keeper's wife and her three children were standing by the open gate, ready to duck profusely in significance of delight in their lord's return. The male bird, as usual, was absent from the nest. Nobody ever saw a man at an entrance lodge.

The avenue of limes was of but thirty years' growth, but there was plenty of good old timber on the broad expanse of meadow-land which Mr. Goring had converted into a park. There was a broad blue lake in the distance, created by the late Mr. Goring, an island in the middle of it, also of his creation; while a fleet of rare and costly foreign aquatic birds of Mr. Goring's importation were sailing calmly on the calm water. And yonder, in the green valley, with a wooded amphitheatre behind it, stood the Abbey, built strictly after the fashion of the fifteenth century, but every block of stone and every lattice obviously of yesterday.

"It wouldn't be half a bad place if it would only mellow down to a sober grayness, instead of being so uncomfortably white and dazzling," said Gerald as they drew near the house.

"It is positively lovely," answered Madoline.

She was looking at the gardens, which thirty years of care and outlay had made about as perfect as gardens of the Italian style can be. They were not such old English gardens as Lord Bacon wrote about. There was nothing wild, no intricate shrubberies, no scope for the imagination, as there was at South Hill. All was planned and filled in with a Dutch neatness. The parterres were laid out in blocks, and in the centre of each rose a fountain from a polished marble basin. Statues by sculptors of note were placed here and there against a background of tall orange-trees, arbutus, or yew. Everything was on a large scale, which suited this palatial Italian manner. Such a garden might have fitly framed the palace of a Medici or a Borgia; nay, in such a garden might Horace have walked by the side of Mæcenas, or Virgil recited a portion of his Æneid to Augustus and Octavia. There was a dignity, a splendour, in these parterres which Daphne thought finer than anything she had seen even at Versailles, whither Madame Tolmache had escorted her English pupils on a certain summer holiday.

"The rose-garden will please you better than this formal pleasaunce, I daresay," said Gerald. "It is on the other side of the house, and consists wholly of grass walks and rose-trees. My dear mother gave her whole mind to the cultivation and improvement of her gardens. I believe she was rather extravagant in this one matter—at least, I have heard my father say so. But I think the result justified her outlay."

"And yet you want to build more hot-houses on my account, Gerald. Surely arrangements that satisfied Lady Geraldine will be good enough for me," said Madoline.

"Oh, one ought to go on improving. Besides, you are fonder of exotics than my mother was. And the rage for church decoration is getting stronger every day. You will have plenty of use for your hot-houses. And now we will go and take a sketchy survey of the house, before we interview the worthy MacCloskie. Has Miss Lawford's

gardener arrived?" Gerald asked of the gentleman in gray, who had occupied the box-seat,
and was again in attendance at the carriage-door,
while a portly butler and a powdered footman,
both of the true English pattern, waited in the
Gothic porch.

"Yes, sir; Mr. MacCloskie is in the housekeeper's-room."

"I hope they have given him luncheon."

"No, sir, thank you, sir. He would take
nothing but a glass of claret and a cigar. He has
taken a stroll round the gardens, sir, so as to be
prepared to give an opinion."

The house was deliciously cool, almost as if ice
had been laid on in the pipes which were used in
winter for hot water. The hall was as profoundly
Gothic as that at Penshurst—it was difficult to
believe that the reek of a log fire piled in the
middle of the stone floor had never gone up through
yonder rafters, that the rude vassals of a feudal
lord had never squatted by the blaze, or slept on
yonder ponderous oaken settles. Nothing was
wanting that should have been there to tell of

an ancient ancestry. Armour that had been battered and dented at Cressy or Bannockburn, or at any rate most skilfully manipulated at Birmingham, adorned the walls. Banners drooped from the rafters; heads of noble stags that had been shot in Arden's primeval wood, spears and battle-axes that had been used in the Crusades, and collected in Wardour Street, gave variety to the artistic decoration of the walls; while tapestry of undoubted antiquity hung before the doorways.

These things had given pleasure to Mr. Giles-Goring, but to his son they were absolutely obnoxious. Yet the father had been so good a father, and had done such honest and useful work in the world before he began to amass this trumpery, that the son had not the heart to dislodge anything.

They went through room after room—all richly furnished, all strictly mediæval: old oak carving collected in the Low Countries; cabinets that reached from floor to ceiling; sideboards large enough to barricade a Parisian boulevard; all the legends of Holy Writ exemplified by the patient

Fleming's chisel; polished oaken floors; panelled walls. The only modern rooms were those at one end of the Abbey, which had been refurnished by Lady Geraldine during her widowhood, and here there was all the lightness and grace of modern upholstery of the highest order. Satinwood furniture and pale-tinted draperies; choice water-colours and choicer porcelain on the walls; books in every available nook.

"How lovely!" cried Daphne, who had not been impressed by the modern mediævalism of the other rooms. "This is where I should like to live."

Lady Geraldine's morning-room looked into the rose-garden. She had not been able to do away with the mullioned windows, but a little glass door —an anachronism, but vastly convenient—had been squeezed into a corner to give her easy access to her favourite garden.

Madoline looked at everything with tender regard. Lady Geraldine had been fond of her and kind to her, and had most heartily approved her son's choice. Tears dimmed Lina's sight as she looked at the familiar room, which seemed so empty without the gracious figure of its mistress.

"I fancied you would like to occupy these rooms by-and-by, Lina," said Gerald.

"I should like it of all things."

"And can you suggest any alterations—any improvements?"

"Gerald, do you think that I would change a thing that your mother cared for? The rooms are lovely in themselves; but were they ever so old-fashioned or shabby, I should like them best as your mother left them."

"Lina, you are simply perfect!" exclaimed Gerald tenderly. "You are just the one faultless woman I have ever met. Chaucer's Grisel was not a diviner creature."

"I hope you are not going to try my sister as that horrid man in the story tried Grisel," cried Daphne, bristling with indignation. "I only wish I had lived in those days, and had the reversion of Count Walter, as a widower. I'd have made him repent his brutality."

"I have no doubt you would have proved

skilful in the art of husband-government," said
Gerald. "But you needn't be alarmed. Much as
I admire Grisel I shan't try to emulate her husband.
I could not leave my wife in agony, and walk away
smiling at the cleverness of my practical joke.
Well, Lina, then it is settled that in these rooms
there is to be no alteration," he added, turning to
Madoline, who had been taking up the volumes
on a little ebony bookstand and looking at their
titles.

"Please make no alteration anywhere. Let the
house be as your father and mother arranged it."

"My sweet conservative! And we are to keep
all the old servants, I conclude. They are all of my
father's and mother's choosing."

"Pray keep them all. If you could any way
find room for MacCloskie, without offending your
head gardener——"

"MacCloskie shall be superintendent of your
own special hot-houses, my darling. It will be an
easy, remunerative place—good wages and plenty
of perquisites."

A grinding of wheels on the gravel, and a

tremendous peal of the bell at the principal entrance proclaimed the advent of a visitor.

"Aunt Rhoda, no doubt," said Gerald. "Let us be sober."

They went back to the hall to greet the new arrival. It was Mrs. Ferrers's youthful groom, a smart young gentleman of the tiger species, who had made that tremendous peal. Mrs. Ferrers's roan ponies were scratching up the gravel; but Mrs. Ferrers was not alone; a gentleman had just dismounted from a fine upstanding bay, and that gentleman was Edgar Turchill.

"So glad to see you here, Aunt Rhoda," cried Gerald. "Why, Turchill, they told me you were in London!"

"Came home last night, rode over to South Hill this morning, overtook Mrs. Ferrers on the way, and——"

"I asked him to come on with me and to join in our round of inspection," said Aunt Rhoda. "I hope I did not do very wrong."

"You did very right. I don't think Turchill feels himself much of a stranger at the Abbey, even though it has been a very inhospitable place for the last year or so. And now before we go in for any more business let's **proceed** to luncheon. Your boat **has** had a most invigorating effect on my appetite, Daphne. I'm simply famished."

"So you came in Daphne's boat. She rows **pretty** well, doesn't she?" asked Edgar, **with a glance** of mingled pride and tenderness at his pupil.

"She might win a cup to-morrow. You have reason to be proud of her."

They all went into the refectory, where, under the lofty open timber roof, a small oval table looked like an island in a sea of Turkey carpet and polished oak flooring.

"It would have served **you** right if we had had the long dinner-table," Gerald said to Daphne, as he passed her with Mrs. Ferrers on his arm.

"I thought we were going to picnic in the park," said Madoline.

"Daphne—— Neither you nor Daphne seemed to care about it," replied Gerald.

"This is a great deal more sensible," remarked Mrs. Ferrers.

"Oh, I don't know; it's awfully jolly to eat one's luncheon under the trees in such weather as this," said Edgar.

"For Mr. Turchill's particular gratification, we will have afternoon-tea in the cloisters," said Gerald. "Blake," to the butler, "let there be tea at half-past four on the grass in the cloisters."

Daphne could eat or drink very little, though Edgar, who sat next to her, was pressing in his offers of lobster mayonnaise, and cold chicken, cutlets, sole à la maitre d'hôtel, Périgord pie. She was looking about her at the portraits on the walls.

Facing her hung Prescott Knight's picture of the man who began his career by wheeling barrows, and who ended it by building mighty viaducts, levelling hills, filling valleys, making the crooked paths straight. It was a brave honest English face, plain, rugged even, the painter having in no wise flattered his sitter; but a countenance that was pleasanter to the eye than many a handsome face. A countenance that promised truth and honour, manliness and warm feelings in its possessor.

Daphne looked from the portrait on the wall to

the present master of the Abbey. No; there was not one point of resemblance between Gerald Goring and his father.

Then she looked at another portrait hanging in the place of honour above the wide Gothic mantelpiece. Lady Geraldine, by Buckner: the picture of an elegant highbred woman of between thirty and forty, dressed in amber satin and black lace, one bare arm lifted to pluck a rose from a lattice, the other hand resting on a marble balustrade, across which an Indian shawl had been flung carelessly. Face and figure were both perfect after their kind—figure tall and willowy, a swan's neck, a proud and pensive countenance, with eyes of the same doubtful colour as Gerald's, the same dreamy look in them. Then Daphne turned her gaze to the other end of the room, where hung the famous Sir Peter Lely, a replica of the well-known picture in Hampton Court, for which replica Mr. Giles-Goring had paid a preposterous price to a poor and proud member of his wife's family, who was lucky enough to possess it. Strange that a single-minded, honest-hearted man like John Giles-Goring should have been proud of his son's descent from a king's mistress, and should have hung the portrait of Felicia, Countess of Heronville, above the desk at which he read family prayers to his assembled household. Yes; Lady Heronville's eyes were like Gerald's, dreamily beautiful.

Everybody at the table had plenty to say, except Daphne. She was absorbed by her contemplation of the pictures. Edgar was concerned at her want of appetite. He tried to entertain her by telling her of the plays and pictures he had seen.

"Your father ought to take you to town before the season is over. There is so much to see," he said; "and though I am told that all the West End tradespeople are complaining, it seems to me that London was never so full as this year. Hyde Park in the morning and afternoon is something wonderful."

"I should like to go to the opera," said Daphne rather listlessly. "Madame Tolmache took us to hear 'Faust' one evening. She said that an occasional visit to the opera was the highest form of cultivation for the youthful mind. I believe she had a box given her by the music-master, and that she turned it to her own advantage that way—charging it in her bills, don't you know. I shall never forget that evening. It was at the end of August, and Paris was wrapped in a white mist, and the air had a breathless, suffocating feeling, and the streets smelt of over-ripe peaches. But when we got out of the jolting fly that took us from the station to the theatre, and went to a box that seemed in the clouds, we had to go up so many stairs to reach it, and the music began, and the curtain went up, it was like being in a new world. I felt as if I were holding my breath all the time. Even Martha Dibb—that stupid, good-natured girl I told you about—seemed spell-bound, and sat with her mouth open, gasping like a fish. Nillson was Marguerite, and Faure was Mephistopheles. I shall remember them to the end of my life."

"You'll hear them again often, I hope. Nillson was singing the other night, when I took my mother to hear Wagner's great opera. The music is quite the rage, I believe; but I don't like it as well as ' Don Giovanni.' "

Luncheon was over by this time—a formal,
ceremonious luncheon, such as Daphne detested. It
was her punishment for having been uncivil last
night when the picnic idea was mooted. And now
they all repaired to the gardens, and perambulated
the parterre, and criticised the statues : Leda with
her swan, Venus with an infant Cupid, Hebe
offering her cup, Ganymede on his eagle—all
the most familiar personages in Lemprière. The
fountains were sending up their rainbow spray
in the blazing afternoon sun. The geraniums, and
calceolarias, and pansies, and petunias, and all the
tribe of begonias, and house-leeks, newly bedded
out, seemed to quiver in the fierce bright light.

"For pity's sake let us get out of this burning
flowery furnace," cried Gerald. "Let's go to the
rose-garden ; it's on the shady side of the house,
and within reach of my mother's favourite tulip-
trees."

The rose-garden was a blessed refuge after that
exposed parterre facing due south. Here there was
velvet turf on which to walk, and here were
trellised screens and arches wreathed with the

yellow clusters of the Celine Forestier, and the Devoniensis. Mrs. Ferrers was a person who always discoursed of flowers by their botanical or fashionable names. She did not call a rose a rose, but went into raptures over a Marguerite de St. Armand, a Garnet Wolseley, a Gloire de Vitry, or an Etienne Levet, as the case might be.

Here, smoking his cigar, which he politely suppressed at their approach, they discovered Mr. MacCloskie, the hard-faced, sandy-haired Scottish gardener.

"You have been taking a look at my grounds, I hear, MacCloskie," Mr. Goring said pleasantly.

"Yes, sir; I've looked about me a bit. I think I've seen pretty well everything."

"And the hot-houses leave room for improvement, I suppose?"

"Well, sir, I'm not wishing to say anything disrespectful to your architect," began MacCloskie, with that deliberation which gave all his speeches an air of superior wisdom, "but if he had tried his hardest to spend the maximum of money in attaining the minimum of space and accommodation

—to say nothing of his ventilation and his heating apparatus, which are just abominable—he couldn't have succeeded better than he has—unconsciously."

"Dear me, Mr. MacCloskie, that's a bad account. And yet the gardeners here have managed to rub on very decently for a quarter of a century, with no better accommodation than you have seen to-day."

"Ay, sir, that's where it is. They've just roobed on, poor fellows. And I can only say that it's very creditable to them to do as well as they have done, and if they're about a quarter of a century behind the times nobody can blame them."

"Then we must build new houses—that's inevitable, I conclude."

"Yes, sir, if you want to grow exotics."

"Yet I used to see a good deal of stephanotis about the rooms in my father's time."

"Ay, there's a fine plant growing in a bit of a glass—shed," said Mr. MacCloskie with ineffable contempt. "Necessity's the mother of invention, Mr. Goring. Your gardeners have done just wonders. But with all deference to you, sir, that kind of thing wouldn't suit me. And if

Miss Lawford has any idea of my coming here by-and-by——" with a respectful glance at his mistress, as he stood at ease, contemplating the spotless lining of his top-hat.

"Miss Lawford would like you to continue in her service when she is Mrs. Goring. Perhaps you will be good enough to give me an exact specification of the space you would require, and the form of house you would suggest. I wish Miss Lawford to be in no way a loser when she exchanges South Hill for Goring Abbey."

"Thank you, sir, you are very good, sir," murmured the Scotchman, as if it were for his gratification the houses were to be built. "This is a very fine place, sir; it would be a pity if it were to be behind the times in any particular."

The head gardener bowed and withdrew, every-one—even Aunt Rhoda—breathing more freely when he had vanished.

"Isn't he too utterly horrid?" asked Daphne. "If there is a being I detest in this world it is he. Were I in Lina's place I should take advantage of my marriage to get rid of him;

but she will just go down to her grave domineered over by that man," concluded Daphne, mimicking MacCloskie's northern tongue.

"He is not the most agreeable person in the world," said Lina; "but he is thoroughly conscientious."

"Did you ever know a disagreeable person who did not set up for being a paragon of honesty?" exclaimed Daphne contemptuously.

They roamed about the rose-garden, which was a lovely place to loiter in upon a summer day, and lingered under the tulip-trees, where there were rustic chairs and a rustic table, and every incentive to idleness. Beyond the tulip-trees there was a shrubbery on the slope of the hill, a shrubbery which sheltered the rose-garden from bleak winds, and made it a thoroughly secluded spot. While the rest of the party sat talking under the big broad-leaved trees, Daphne shot off to explore the shrubbery. The first thing that attracted her attention was a large wire cage among the laurels.

"Is that an aviary?" she asked.

"No," answered Gerald, rising and going over to her. "These are my father's antecedents."

He pulled away the laurel branches which had spread themselves in front of the cage, and Daphne saw that it contained only a shabby old barrow, a pickaxe, and shovel.

"Those were the stock-in-trade with which my father began his career," he said. "I don't believe he had even the traditional half-crown. I've no doubt if he had possessed such a coin his mates would have made him spend it on beer. He began life, a barefooted, ignorant lad, upon a railroad in the North of England; and before his fortieth birthday he was one of the greatest contractors and one of the best-informed men of his time; but he never mastered the right use of the aspirate, and he never could bring himself to wear gloves. It was his fancy to keep those old tools of his, and to take his visitors to look at them, after they had gone the round of house and gardens."

"I hope you are proud of him," said Daphne, with a bright penetrating glance which seemed to pierce Mr. Goring's soul. "I should hate you if

I thought that, even for one moment in your life, you could feel ashamed of such a father."

"Then I'm afraid I must endure your hate," said Gerald. "No; I have never felt ashamed of my father: he was the dearest, kindest, most unselfish, most indulgent father that ever spoiled an unworthy son. But I have occasionally felt ashamed of that barrow, when it has been exhibited and explained to a new acquaintance, and I have seen that the new acquaintance thought the whole thing—the mock mediæval abbey, and the barrow, and my dear simple-hearted dad—one stupendous joke."

"I should be more ashamed of Felicia, Countess of Heronville, than of that barrow, if I were you," exclaimed Daphne, flushed and indignant.

"You little radical! Mistress Felicia was by no means an exemplary person, but she was one of the loveliest women at Charles's court, where lovely women congregated by common consent, while all the ugly ones buried themselves at their husbands' country seats, and thought that some fiery comet must be swooping down upon the world because of wickedness in high places. Don't be too hard upon poor Lady Heronville. She died in the zenith of her charms, while quite a young woman."

"Do you think she ought to be pitied for that?" demanded Daphne. "Why, it was the brightest fate Heaven could give her. The just punishment for her evil ways would have been a long loveless old age, and to see her beauty fade day by day, and to know that the world she loved despised and forgot her.

> Whom the gods love die young was said of old;
> And many deaths do they escape by this.

"Where did you find those lines, little one?"

"In a book we used to read aloud at Madame Tolmache's, 'Gems from Byron.'"

"Oh, I see! Mere chippings, diamond dust. I was afraid you'd been at the Koh-i-noor itself."

"Are we to have some tea, Gerald?" asked Madoline, crossing to them and looking at her watch as she came. "It is half-past four, and we must be going home soon."

"To the cloisters, ladies and gentlemen, to all that there is of the most mediæval in the Abbey."

They passed under a Gothic archway and found themselves on a square green lawn, in the midst of which was another fountain in a genuine old marble basin, a Roman relic dug up thirty years ago in the peninsula of Portland. A cloistered walk surrounded this grass-plot. A striped awning had been put up beside the fountain, and under this the tea-table was spread.

"Now, Lina, let us see if you can manage that ponderous tea-kettle," said Gerald.

"It is the handsomest I ever saw," sleepily remarked Mrs. Ferrers, who had found the afternoon somewhat dreary, since nobody had seemed to want her advice about anything. "But I must confess that I prefer the Rector's George the Second silver, and old Swansea cups and saucers, to the highest exemplars of modern art."

END OF VOL. I.

CHARLES DICKENS AND EVANS, CRYSTAL PALACE PRESS.

www.ingramcontent.com/pod-product-compliance
Lightning Source LLC
Chambersburg PA
CBHW020953030726
47496CB00005B/1486